Advance praise for
We Were Beautiful

"*We Were Beautiful* is a profound story of relearning how to love and live in the aftermath of trauma. Mia's journey into a new identity celebrates the healing power of friendship and the enduring beauty of survivors."

MARIE MARQUARDT, author of *The Radius of Us*, *Dream Things True*, and *Flight Season*

"A deftly crafted novel by an author with a genuine talent for holding her reader's rapt attention from beginning to end, *We Were Beautiful*, by Heather Hepler, is unreservedly recommended for school and community library YA Fiction collections."

MIDWEST BOOK REVIEW

We were Beautiful

We were Beautiful

HEATHER HEPLER

BLINK

BLINK

We Were Beautiful
Copyright © 2019 by Heather Hepler

Requests for information should be addressed to:
Blink, *3900 Sparks Dr. SE, Grand Rapids, Michigan 49546*

ISBN 978-0-310-76864-7 (audio)

ISBN 978-0-310-76643-8 (print)

ISBN 978-0-310-76638-4 (ebook)

Library of Congress Cataloging-in-Publication Data

Names: Hepler, Heather, author.
Title: We were beautiful / Heather Hepler.
Description: Grand Rapids, Michigan: Blink, [2019] | Summary: Fifteen-year-old
    Mia's scarred face is a constant reminder of the car crash that killed her sister,
    but a summer at her grandmother's Manhattan apartment and new friends
    help her find happiness again.
Identifiers: LCCN 2018049881 (print) | LCCN 2018054159 (ebook) | ISBN
    9780310766384 (ebook) | ISBN 9780310766438 (softcover)
Subjects: | CYAC: Disfigured persons--Fiction. | Grief—Fiction. | Guilt—Fiction. |
    Friendship—Fiction. | Grandmothers—Fiction. | New York (N.Y.)—Fiction.
Classification: LCC PZ7.H4127 (ebook) | LCC PZ7.H4127 We 2019 (print) | DDC
[Fic]—dc23
LC record available at https://lccn.loc.gov/2018049881

Interior design: Denise Froehlich

Printed in the United States of America

19 20 21 22 23 / LSC / 10 9 8 7 6 5 4 3 2 1

For my mother, who always believes.

Chapter One

The only sounds in the kitchen are the hum of the refrigerator, the scratch of a knife across toast, and the low murmuring of the radio tuned to NPR. My father sits across the table from me in our tiny kitchen. He's buttering his toast, one bite at a time. Butter, bite, butter, bite. I want to ask him why he doesn't just butter the whole thing at once, but that would mean talking to him. And I know he'd rather I didn't do that.

I stir a fourth teaspoon of sugar into my tea. The station is quiet for a moment, and then there's Rachel's voice, filling the kitchen like it used to every morning. But instead of coming from her usual chair across from me, her voice spills from the radio. And instead of her stream of thoughts ranging from why Grape-Nuts cereal contains neither grapes nor nuts to where they get the extra pulp for the country-style orange juice my father likes, she's talking about the upcoming pledge drive and why we should support our local public radio station.

My father and I both look at the radio. Then he looks back at his toast and I look at the sugar bowl, trying to decide if I should add another spoonful of sugar to my already too-sweet tea. My sister, the actress. Her one paying job was a voice-over for the local radio station.

"You all packed?" Dad asks, as if nothing happened. I nod, but then remember he doesn't look at me anymore.

"Yeah," I say. I glance at the one duffle bag I left beside the kitchen door. "I still don't see why I have to—"

My father sighs, silencing me. He pushes away from the table and walks over to the sink. "Mia," he says. His voice is strained, as if just saying my name aloud is painful for him. "We've been over this. You can't stay here by yourself."

"But I'm fifteen," I say.

He sighs again and turns to wash his plate in the sink. I touch the scar on my cheek. The doctor said it will flatten out in time, but it's still raised and bumpy, like a rope of red licorice stuck to the side of my face. My fingertip traces it from where it starts at my hairline to where it ends near my collarbone, neatly bisecting my eye and my mouth as it meanders down toward my neck.

The water shuts off. I look up to see my father staring at me, and my hand freezes. He turns away and grabs his keys from a nail driven into the doorframe.

"Mia," he says. "We both need some time."

"For what?" I ask. I'm not being argumentative. I just really don't understand why he feels leaving will somehow fix what is broken between us.

"I don't know," he says, walking over to where my duffle lies. He lifts my bag and pushes open the screen door without looking back at me. "Don't forget your camera," he says. The door snaps shut behind him, leaving me alone in the kitchen.

I sit and stare at the untouched mug of tea in front of me until I hear his truck start up and then the sound of tires on gravel as he pulls out of the barn and around to the back door. As I stand up, my necklace falls free from the collar of my shirt. I quickly stuff it back inside, feeling its familiar weight against my chest. The silver is warm against my skin, but the chain chafes my neck. My father honks once, impatient to get going. Impatient to get me gone.

I quickly wash out my mug and leave it in the dish drainer. I walk out onto the porch, not bothering to lock the door behind me. With my mother and sister long gone and my father and I driving away, anything we had that was worth stealing has already been taken. I start down the steps, but pause before reaching the bottom. My camera. I wasn't going to bring it. I haven't even touched it in almost a year, but thinking about things lost makes me afraid to leave it. Too many things have disappeared without warning over the last year. I head back inside and slide it from the shelf above the rows of chicken noodle soup and canned beans that make up most of our meals. It's heavier than I remember.

I hurry back outside and across the driveway to where my father is sitting in our truck, my duffle bag on the seat beside him. I yank the passenger side door open, wincing as it screeches, and climb inside. We bump out onto the road, picking up speed as we hit the asphalt.

As we drive, I find myself searching the fog over the lake for Rachel's bright pink kayak. I bite the inside of my cheek to make myself look away. My sister's boat is not on the water. It's hanging from the rafters of our barn, its fuchsia glow muted by months of gray dust.

After fifteen minutes of silence, we pull up to the curb in front of the train station. I didn't expect my father to walk me in and wait with me, but he doesn't even offer. He simply puts the truck in park and shuts it off, then leans toward me. For a moment, I think he's going to hug me, but he's only shifting so he can get to his wallet. He pulls out two twenties and lays them on the duffle between us.

"I sent Veronica a check," he says. "To cover any expenses."

I pick up the money and push it into the front pocket of my jeans, not sure if I'm supposed to thank him.

"Listen," he begins, but he doesn't say anything else. He just clutches the steering wheel and stares through the windshield.

A speaker hung above the platform crackles to life. The voice echoes off the building, making it hard to hear the announcement, but I hear *New York* and *departing*.

"I should go," I say, not so much because I'm ready, but because the inside of the truck is hot and my father feels too close and too far away at the same time.

"I'll try to call you," he says. "But I don't know what our schedule will be like." I wonder if he realizes it's almost the exact thing my mother told me the last time she called. The only difference is that his schedule involves deep-water diving and weapons training, while my mother's schedule is filled with praying and baking fruitcake.

I push the door open and drop to the pavement, then turn and slide my duffle toward me. "I'll see you in . . . August," I say. I can barely get the word out. August. Months away.

He clenches his jaw and takes a deep breath before nodding. I stand there, watching the side of his face as he turns the key and the truck roars to life. I sling my bag over my shoulder and cradle my camera in my hands before I take a step back and push the door shut. I watch him pull away from the curb and away from me.

He doesn't wave or look back. Neither do I.

I walk through the station, past the cracked Formica chairs and vending machines stuffed with ranch Corn Nuts and Funyuns. The smells of urine and bleach battle for dominance near the bathrooms. Out on the platform, I wait in the shadow of the building as people board the train.

Only when everyone is aboard but me do I move into the sunlight, careful to keep my hair draped across my face. I step into the closest car, praying there will be a window seat, something on the right-hand side of the train. I have to walk through two cars before I find an empty row. I slide into the seat next to the window, leaving my bag beside me, hoping people will take the hint I want to sit alone.

I always try to sit to the right of people because from the left, I look totally normal. Red hair, pale skin, green eyes. But if you stand to the right of me, it's a different story. My face is ruined. The doctor I was seeing in Boston told me that in a few more months, we could do another round of surgeries. More reconstruction. Try to make my eyes line up better. But he wants some time to pass to allow me to heal.

I slide the book I brought with me free of my duffle. It's one I've had for a long time, a book about fairy tales. My mom found it at the Old Port Book Shoppe during one of our afternoons scouring the used bookstores. She actually said *Score!* out loud, like she'd just found a hundred-dollar bill wedged between the pages. I'd rolled my eyes at her, but I couldn't help smiling. We sat on the floor in the hot, dusty shop with our shoulders touching and the book spread across our laps. We stayed there, looking at the illustrations and reading bits aloud to each other. The sky was beginning to darken by the time we left, the plastic bag with our treasure inside clutched in my right hand and my mother's warm hand in my left.

It's hard to read with the train lurching. I have to stop every few minutes to let my eyes rest. My vision becomes blurry when my eyes get fatigued, particularly the right one. That's another thing the doctor is hoping will go away. Another thing to heal.

I look up when I feel someone staring at me. It's a little girl a few rows in front of me. Her eyes are wide and her brow furrowed.

"Lexi, stop staring," a woman whispers.

I'm not sure why her mother is bothering to say anything now. Lexi has been staring at me nonstop ever since they boarded the train over half an hour ago. Now she's watching me with a lollipop stuck in her mouth. Lexi slides down in her seat a little and looks away until her mother returns to her magazine. Then she's right back to staring at me. She crunches the last of her lollipop, then gets up to throw the stick away. Her mother glances at her briefly and nods. Instead of putting her stick in the trash can closest to them, however, Lexi walks down the aisle toward me. I duck my head and pretend to read. Lexi stops in the aisle next to my row.

"What happened to your face?" she asks. She tilts her head, curious. It's nothing like the whispers behind hands and open sneers I've been navigating for the last few months.

I look over at her mother, who is still flipping through her magazine. I turn and face Lexi straight on, thinking that if she gets a good look at me, she'll go away. Her eyes widen slightly, but she holds her ground. Normally I would turn away if someone looked at me like that, but Lexi's not staring at me like I'm a monster—more like I'm a puzzle she's trying to figure out.

She leans toward me. "Did a witch do that to you?"

"No," I say, hoping she doesn't press me. I don't really want to have that conversation with a six-year-old who has cherry lollipop smeared all over her cheeks.

Lexi looks at me. "I'll bet it was," she says. The certainty in her voice catches me off guard. "I'll bet that's part of the spell. You can't tell anyone about it. Was it a poison apple?" she asks. I shake my head. "Did you poke your finger on a spiggle?" she asks.

"A spindle?" She bobs her head. "No," I say. "I just wasn't careful."

Lexi seems shocked by this. I don't blame her. My story wouldn't make a very good fairy tale. No dragons or fairies or jealous stepsisters. She chews on the end of her lollipop stick, thinking.

"Are you going to find your fairy godmother?" she asks.

"No," I say. "I'm meeting my grandmother." I want to add that I'm meeting her for the first time, but Lexi is shaking her head.

"You have to find your fairy godmother," she says. "Only she can break the spell." I start to say something cynical, something about how magic isn't real, but the look in Lexi's eyes stops me. She'll figure it out for herself soon enough.

Finally, Lexi's mom notices her daughter hasn't returned

and hustles down the aisle toward us. She grabs Lexi's hand and offers me what I'm sure is meant to be an apologetic smile, but it seems more like a horrified grimace.

"I'm so sorry—" she begins, but the way she says it, I'm not sure if she's sorry about Lexi or about my face. Maybe both. She pulls Lexi back to their seats.

"Good luck," Lexi says. She plants her feet, forcing her mother to stop. "Just remember your fairy godmother."

I nod as her mother drags her away. I flip open the book in my lap, trying to find my place. Staring up at me is an artist's sketch of Cinderella. She is dressed in rags and is shoeless, kneeling in the cold ashes of the fireplace. She is looking through a window toward the flower-filled gardens beyond. But the window is shut, the iron latch is tight. There seems to be no hope that she will one day walk in the sun.

The speaker over my head sputters to life with our arrival announcements. We are told to gather our things and be ready to "detrain," which I didn't even know was a word. Lexi and her mother are already standing in the aisle. Her mother offers me one more pained smile as if just looking at me is hurting her. Lexi waves as they step off the train. I wave back.

I wait until the car is clear before walking down the aisle to the open door. The smell of the city hits me first— dark and smoky and slightly moldy. I walk past towering columns of concrete toward the escalator leading up to the rest of the station, where a woman I've never met before is waiting.

I'm almost to the escalator when I hear a low whistle. I know I shouldn't look over, but I do.

"Hey, beautiful," a guy with dark curly hair says. I stare at him for a moment too long. The guy sneers at me. "I wasn't talking to you, Freak Show." His friends all crack up. High fives all the way around.

Of course you weren't, I think. I step onto the escalator and ride it up to the top, hoping they don't see the blush staining my cheeks. When I reach the main part of the station, I look around, wondering how I'll figure out which woman is my grandmother. Luckily, I don't have to. A tall woman with graying hair, with strands that hint it was once red, walks right up to me. She sticks out her hand, making me juggle my camera so that I can shake it.

"Veronica Thompson," she says, giving my hand a squeeze that feels more like she's checking the ripeness of a peach.

"Mia Hopkins," I say.

My grandmother studies me for a long moment before giving a barely perceptible nod. *You'll do*, it says. *Maybe.* Then she turns away from me and walks toward a wall of glass doors that will take us out onto the street. It's clear I'm to follow.

We're in a cab and pulling into traffic before I have a chance to look around. Cars press in on us from every side and buildings march into the distance as far as I can see. Our cab driver keeps switching lanes, looking for the perfect path through the snarl of traffic.

Veronica instructs him on where to turn and what roads to take. He nods, but ignores her direction. Finally, she turns to me. "You're late," she says, like it's my fault the train wasn't on time.

"Oh," I say. Because what else is there? All my life, my mom told us what a monster her mother was, how she was so controlling. So condescending. So cold. How she was incapable of loving anyone other than herself.

I look at her out of the corner of my eye as our taxi weaves through traffic on the way to her apartment. I can see my mother in the line of her jaw, but I see my sister in her eyes. The cab barely slows as it turns, making me slide over the slick seat and toward my grandmother. She doesn't even glance in my direction.

Our cab speeds down a shaded street lined with trees and then slams to a stop in front of a bank of trash cans crowding the curb. I push open my door as far as it will go and squeeze out onto the sidewalk. My grandmother waits for the driver to get out and open her door. I can tell by the look on his face he's thinking that's not in his job description, but the press of bills into his hand leaves him smiling.

I stare up at the building I assume will be my home for the next couple of months. A set of stairs leads up from the sidewalk to the front door. My grandmother walks around the back of the taxi and heads up the wide brick steps. A man in a uniform pops out of the front door like a life-sized jack-in-a-box.

"Good afternoon, Ms. Thompson," he says. My grandmother nods curtly at him. He looks past her to me. "This must be your granddaughter."

I look up. His eyes open a millimeter wider at the sight of my face, but he's clearly a professional. "Afternoon, miss," he says without missing a beat. I bob my head in hello before following my grandmother inside.

The ride up in the elevator is the same as the ride in the cab, except this time we're traveling vertically and there's nothing to look at but the numbered lights above the door. The doors slide open on the fourth floor. I follow my grandmother to the right and wait while she rummages in her bag for the key.

She pushes the door open and we step inside. After a short hallway, there is a living room with floor-to-ceiling windows and shelves stuffed with books.

She places her purse and keys on a table and leads me farther into the apartment. "That's my room," she says, pointing at a closed door, "and you're in here."

I notice she doesn't say it's *my* room, and I soon understand why. The door barely opens wide enough for her to squeeze through, and as I slide in after her, leaving my duffle bag in the hall, it's immediately obvious why the door won't open more than a dozen inches. Other than a bed that is wedged in the corner, the room is filled floor to ceiling with old books. The earthy reds and deep greens line the shelves and spill onto the floor, and their musty smell reminds me of my mother. She used to hide book purchases from my father like other women might hide new shoes or an expensive new purse.

I walk over to one of the shelves and study some of the titles as my grandmother clears her throat. "I talked with Mrs. Brunelli. She said you should stop by at four tomorrow morning," she says before sliding out the door.

"Wait," I say, turning from the books to my grand-mother. "Stop by where?"

I don't ask the seven other questions I have, leading with *Who the heck is Mrs. Brunelli? And four a.m.?*

"The diner on the corner," she replies, like I should somehow already have this information. "I got you a job."

"Oh," I say. I touch the scar on the side of my face, a nervous habit I've developed over the past few months. The therapist I was seeing said it was normal for people who've been in accidents to touch their scars. *It grounds you,* she said.

"I don't want you lying around here all summer," my grandmother says, but what I hear is: *I don't want you here all summer.* And all I can think is something Rachel used to always say: *Amen to that, sister.* Because it seems she doesn't want me here as much as I don't want to be here. Though instead of being funny, it just makes me feel more alone.

My grandmother squeezes back through the door, but stops in the hall and pokes her head back in. "I suspect you'll want to make yourself presentable before Mass." It's more of a command than a suggestion. "It's at seven o'clock."

"Mass?" I ask, but she doesn't elaborate.

She disappears, but then she's back. Again. "I'm glad you're here," she says, but her words are clipped and fast like she's trying to run away from them. She stands in the doorway, waiting. I know I should say I'm glad to be here too, but I'm not. I settle for something else.

"What should I call you?" I ask. It's a valid question. She doesn't answer immediately, and I wonder if she's running through the options: Mimi, Granny, Nana, Gram.

"Ms. Thompson seems too formal," she says. My eyes widen only slightly. *You think?* "Since we're family, I suppose Veronica would be appropriate."

I nod. Veronica. Fabulous. She pulls the door shut after her, cutting off anything I might have thought to say. I sigh and sink onto the edge of the bed. Hung above my bed is a crucifix. I remember what my mother used to say about growing up Catholic. *They like to keep Christ on the cross where they can keep an eye on him.*

I lie back and stare up at the ceiling above my bed. There's another cross hung over my bed. This one is plain wood, wrapped in barbed wire. I pull out my necklace and look at the locket, watching the light play across it as I hold it up. Then I close my eyes. I should rest, but I'm afraid I'll fall asleep. And I'll do just about anything not to sleep. The therapist said my dreams will probably intensify at first as my memory improves. She said they'd fade after a while, *as my psyche assimilates the trauma.* I have my doubts.

The weird thing about my dreams is that there aren't

any images—just sounds. Like watching a movie with my eyes closed. Sometimes I try to open my eyes because I want to see, need to see. But other times, I'm grateful for the safety of the darkness.

I sit up, wrap my arms around my legs, and lean my forehead against my knees. In this position, if I start to drift off I'll fall over and wake up. I sit there with my eyes closed until my grandmother—I mean Veronica—knocks on the door and tells me it's time to leave.

Chapter Two

"*Your* problem is, you lack confidence," Veronica says. I nod, trying to keep up as I follow her down the sidewalk leading to her church. "That and you slouch." I nod again and try to stand a little bit taller.

I have to jog a few steps to keep from losing her in the crowd that shares the sidewalk with us. The sidewalk is packed. Tall people. Short people. Yelling people. Texting people. Purple-haired people, and one almost-naked person wearing silver sparkle short shorts and playing an accordion.

"Keep up," Veronica says over her shoulder. I hurry across the intersection, stepping away from the front of a cab a nanosecond before the light changes. I feel the blast of heat from his engine on the backs of my knees as he passes. I frown at the back of Veronica's head as she pushes past a couple wearing matchy sweats. It's not so much that she's fast, it's that nothing and no one gets in her way. Confidence is not something she lacks. She walks purposefully, with her arms swinging. More than one person has already gotten his ribs clipped as she walks by.

"Sorry," I mumble as I walk past the matchy couple. That was a mistake. The woman looks at me with a smile, as if to say she understands difficult grandmothers, but her face morphs into shock and quickly into pity. People always do that when they see my face. I hate that last bit. I don't want anyone feeling sorry for me.

I try to walk close to the buildings and keep my hair hanging over my right cheek. Only a young girl wearing a pink shirt with a unicorn on it smiles at me. For a second, I think it's Lexi and I smile back. I'm so focused on the magic wand she's holding in her hand that I end up running right into the back of my grandmother, who has stopped at the corner.

"Sorry," I say again. It's become like a mantra to me. *I'm sorry.* "Do you go to church every week?" I ask as we cross the street and walk down the block toward a giant stone building.

"I go every day," Veronica says.

And sure enough, the schedule posted on the front of the church states that they do, in fact, have services every day. Veronica sees me looking at the sign. "I go twice on Sundays." She looks at me and adds, "I don't expect you to go every day," but the tone of her voice suggests she will find me lacking if I choose *not* to go.

I do some quick math in my head. In two weeks, Veronica goes to church more than I have in my entire life. My family only went on Christmas Eve. It was as much a part of our Christmas as the stockings or the tree or the light-up reindeer we used to put in our yard. I loved it—the candles, the poinsettias, the music. I didn't even mind that it was the one time of the year my mother insisted I wear a dress.

Veronica didn't make me wear a dress, but she did insist on something other than jeans and sneakers. I have one skirt, but I don't have any shoes except my Chucks and a pair of hiking boots, so Veronica loaned me a pair of her shoes. So not only am I wearing sensible, old lady shoes, I'm wearing shoes that are a size too small, which is why I'm almost limping by the time we get to the steps leading up to the church.

Veronica waits at the base of the steps for me to catch up with her. When I draw even, she starts ascending, expecting me to follow. But I stop for a moment to let my feet rest, and take in my surroundings. I have to lean my head all the way back to see the crucifix hanging over the door. The figure is nearly the same as the one mounted over my bed, but on this one Christ's eyes are open, staring at me. This time I feel like it's *him* keeping an eye on *me*.

"Mia?" Veronica says from where she's waiting for me again; this time at the top of the stairs. I climb slowly because my feet hurt, but also because I'm becoming increasingly nervous about entering the church. Even though I don't believe in God anymore, something about going inside *his house*, as Veronica keeps putting it, makes me uneasy. My anxiety increases as Veronica instructs me to dip my fingers in the holy water and cross myself. It's that I think my skin is going to suddenly start bubbling when the water touches me, like I'm some sort of vampire, but it feels hypocritical. Veronica waits while I wet my fingers and make a weak cross on my front.

We walk into the main part of the church, where not more than two dozen people are kneeling in the rows. Veronica dips at the end of the aisle and crosses herself again. I follow her into the row. No bowing. No crossing. She folds a little cushioned bench down from the row in front of us and kneels on it before closing her eyes. I watch as her lips move silently as I kneel beside her, then look toward the front, where rows of candles flicker. About half the candles are lit. Every once in a while, someone will walk forward to light another candle and stand with their head bowed for a few moments before returning to kneel again in the pew.

A part of me is jealous of that simplicity. Light a candle. Say a prayer. It feels like the same thing everyone else has promised. Surgery. Counseling. Time. Like all I need to do is follow these simple steps and I'll be fine.

A side door opens. Everyone stands up as the priest walks to the front of the room. We stay standing while he says a bunch of stuff about repentance and forgiveness and penance and grace. And the whole time I'm thinking, *If only you knew.*

Then the priest is holding a covered dish, and he starts talking about bread and wine and bloodshed. The words repeat in my head. *Wine. Bloodshed. Wine. Bloodshed.*

The church is hot, and the incense snaking through the air is sweet, almost cloying. We stand and Veronica nods toward the front. I start to shake my head, but she grabs my hand.

"Just put your arms across your chest," she whispers as we join the line of people. I try, but I don't do it right and she has to correct me. I take deep breaths, hoping that will help clear my head. But all the deep breaths send more of the incense into my lungs and straight into my brain. The line slowly moves forward. I keep my eyes fixed on the flickering candles.

When we finally make it to the front, Veronica steps forward, accepting the wafer, then moves to the side. The priest nods encouragingly at me, but my head is spinning and I can barely respond. Memories press at the edges of my mind. The priest makes the sign of the cross over me and motions for me to step toward my grandmother. I try to move, but my legs feel rubbery. Then everything turns green and suddenly the floor is rushing up at me. The last thing I remember is laughing, because for one crazy moment all I can think is that I'm shedding the blood too, but instead of it covering sin, it's just covering the front of my skirt and my sensible, too-tight shoes. And then it's simply dark.

Veronica says we'll get a cab to take us back to her apartment, but I tell her I'd like to walk. The fresh air will do me good. I apologize several times on the way home, although I'm not entirely clear on why I should be sorry. I mean, I passed out. The fact that I cracked my head on the marble floor and am wearing most of the Communion wine down my front seems like penance enough for whatever sin I supposedly committed. I shake my head a little, trying to dislodge all that church-speak out of my brain. It's awful enough that I just embarrassed myself in front of dozens of people and almost knocked a priest to the ground. I can barely stand the added humiliation that Veronica seems determined to lay on me.

"Your blood sugar is probably low," Veronica says. "You need to eat more. Or maybe you're dehydrated." We walk up the steps into her building. The doorman nods at us as we pass. "Are you sleeping okay?" she asks me.

"Not really," I say. She presses her lips together and nods as if she just solved my problem.

"I'm just glad you're feeling better," is all Veronica says to me on the ride up in the elevator. Once we are in her apartment, she tells me she's going to lie down. "If you're hungry after your shower, there's some food in the refrigerator," she says. The not-so-subtle reminder that I'm filthy hangs in the air between us. "There are the spare keys and a map to Brunelli's Diner," she says, nodding toward the kitchen counter.

I look at the piece of paper laid there. The grid lines are so straight; it's obvious she used a ruler to draw in the streets. She even inked in the newsstand on the corner, complete with its striped awning.

"Thanks," I say, looking up at her. "What will I be doing?" I ask.

"They'll tell you," she says. Veronica nods, then turns and walks down the hall. She pauses in front of her bedroom door. "Do I need to wake you in the morning, or can you get yourself up?"

"I'll set my alarm," I say.

"Very well. Good night, then." She steps into her bedroom, pushing the door shut behind her.

I glance down at my skirt, which is still stiff and damp with wine. I decide that Veronica is completely correct. I could definitely use a cleanup.

After my shower, I change into normal clothes and head into the kitchen. I decide to eat some dinner, because the only things I've had all day are the bruised apple and half of the granola bar I packed in my duffle. I pull open the refrigerator, expecting to see a jar of peanut butter and a loaf of bread, but there on the shelf is a plate covered with plastic, containing a perfect mound of mashed potatoes pushed up against a slice of what looks like meatloaf.

A small dish of peas sits beside the plate. It appears home-made, but empty cartons in the trash tell me it's takeout. I debate whether to heat the food, but I'm afraid the micro-wave might damage the china.

I find a fork and carry my food to the table. I take a few bites of potato, but quickly realize that despite not having eaten much, I can't make the food go down. I replace the plastic wrap over the plate and slide it back into the refrigerator. As I do, I notice my arms have these weird pink stains on them. Rationally, I know it's from the wine, but my mind only sees blood. And then it happens.

Rachel is crumpled against the passenger door, her hair falling across her face. Her pale skin is streaked with blood.

I slide down the cabinet and sit on the cold floor. I take deep breaths, trying to make it go away, but it won't. It just keeps playing in my head, a loop. Rachel and the broken window and the blood. Over and over. The psychiatrist talked about triggers, seemingly random events that will jog something free in my brain. She said I'd probably remember things in spurts. Images without sequence or context. But she didn't warn me about this.

"Stop," I whisper. "Please."

Finally, it does. I sit, shivering on the floor until my heart slows and my breathing stops coming in ragged gasps. When I feel strong enough, I stand and hold on to the counter until the buzzy feeling in my head goes away. Once I feel steady enough, I walk over to the window and look out, trying to see the sky in between the buildings. It's dark, but not the kind of dark I'm used to. When night falls in Maine, light just ceases to exist. Rachel and I used to sit on the back porch in the evening, and if we tilted our heads back, all we could see were stars. So many that it looked like a bowl of them had been upended over Earth.

Like holes to heaven, Rachel used to tell me.

Here in New York, I can't see any stars at all. Just the bright city lights and the darkness beyond.

Chapter Three

The good news is that I don't have to wear a uniform like I did when I worked at Boom's Ice Cream last summer. (Apparently Boom thought that baseball caps with huge brown pom-poms on top would sell ice cream.) At the diner, I can simply wear jeans and a T-shirt. The bad news is I assumed Veronica got me the early shift so I wouldn't have to see anyone. And that might have been true where I used to live in Downeast Maine, but that's not true here in Manhattan. Even though I've been at the restaurant for only half an hour, I've already seen eight people, and those are just the people who actually came into the kitchen. There have been another dozen or so in the front, stacking newspapers, bringing in produce, and delivering napkins and straws and those little paper thingies you use to grab donuts so you don't have to touch them with your bare hands.

I stand to one side, waiting for some kind of direction. The kitchen is dominated by a giant chrome table. Above it, hanging from hooks, are dozens of utensils—spoons and whisks and ladles of every size. Flats of strawberries and crates of eggs dominate one end of the counter, while the other is filled with wheels and logs of cheese.

"Hey," a man from the doorway calls. I glance around, but no one pays him any attention. He sees me looking and nods. "You," he says. "You need more butter?" I shrug and he rolls his eyes. "What about anchovy cream cheese?" A tiny woman comes out of the office with a phone wedged between her shoulder and her ear.

"Carlos," she says, looking at the man. "Forty butter and no cream cheese." He nods and heads back outside. Then she turns to me. She puts the phone down on the counter and smiles. "You're Mia," she says, taking my hand. I nod. "Call me Nonna." She gives me an apron and shows me where I can store my camera. I'm still not planning to use it, but I wasn't about to leave it in the apartment with my grandmother. That's one of the downsides of a digital camera. All you have to do is turn it on to see any photos I've taken.

Then Nonna tells me I have to pull my hair back.

"Health code," she says when I hesitate. I haven't worn my hair back in almost a year, but before I can explain she hands me a rubber band from one of the desk drawers, and checks an invoice while I try to pull as much of my hair into a ponytail as possible. Nonna looks at me for about two seconds, and then shows me where I can wash my hands.

"Your first job every morning is to fill the coffee makers." She leads me to the front where no fewer than twelve coffee makers are lined up along the back wall like an army of caffeinated soldiers.

"Which ones are decaf?" I ask, looking for green rims on some of the pots.

Nonna starts laughing. "Decaf," she says, laughing even harder. "Aren't you precious?" She wipes at her eyes with the hem of her apron, then shows me where I can find the filters and how to work the grinder. Nonna moves along to show me the baking list that's pinned on the doorframe leading into the kitchen. I start scanning it before she pulls it down and leads me back inside the kitchen. "We'll start with rugelach," she says, clapping her hands together.

She instructs me to haul out bins of sugar and flour and a huge tub of cinnamon, then puts me to work zesting oranges while she drops huge slabs of cream cheese into the stand mixer. Nonna talks the whole time she's working, telling me how happy she is that I came to help this summer while her daughter-in-law, who usually works as the baker's helper, is out with a new baby.

"Tiny little thing. Not much bigger than a loaf of bread." I assume she means the baby and not the daughter-in-law. In the time it takes us to slide the last of the pastries into the ovens and start on the turnovers, I've learned the whole

Brunelli family tree. It seems that other than one of the waitresses (and now me), everyone at Brunelli's is related.

"Nine children," Nonna says. She laughs when she sees my eyes go huge. "Twenty-seven grandchildren. Wait, no, twenty-eight. I almost forgot little Gracie."

I can't even imagine having that big of a family. The truth is, I can barely remember what it's like to have any family at all—big, little, or otherwise. Thankfully Nonna doesn't ask about my family. Maybe knowing my grandmother is enough information for anyone.

I concentrate on using a fork to press the edges of the turnovers together so the apple filling won't leak out. I steal a look at the clock hanging over the sink. Almost six. Nonna didn't say when I would be finished. I had hoped to be out before the diner opened, but looking at the list she gave me, it's obvious that's not going to happen. Nonna sees the look on my face.

She puts a floury hand on my arm and smiles. "Don't worry, Mia-honey. It just takes a little while to get the hang of it." She takes the fork from me and crimps the edges of half a dozen turnovers faster than I could have done one. "And don't worry about that," she says, nodding toward the list. "I have someone coming in to help you."

Nonna instructs me to make sure the coffee machines are all on. I walk to the front, keeping my chin tucked so that my face stays a little hidden. Joey, the guy who works the grill and who Nonna told me is still *unmarried* (she crossed herself as she said it), flips the sign on the door to Open and turns the catch, unlocking it. He barely steps back from the door before people start streaming in. I start back toward the kitchen, but a man in a suit starts yelling at me to give him his usual. Grace, who Nonna warned me to be careful of (without explanation), elbows me aside and begins pulling pastries from the racks under the counter. She starts firing words at me that I assume are Italian. I stand there, not sure what to do.

Grace turns on me, her face red. "Get. The. Coffee."

This I understand. I spend the next hour pouring coffee into cups and refilling the machines as they empty.

I quickly learn the difference between a cannoli and a cream horn, which look similar except the horns narrow at one end and are soft. I also learn the names of the other three people working the front. Mary is short and round and seems afraid of everyone and everything. Gina smiles a lot and flirts with everyone who comes in. I don't really get a sense of Rosie, who stays at the far end of the counter ringing up everyone's order.

"Hey, new girl! How 'bout a cookie?" someone shouts.

I keep spooning coffee into a filter until Gina nudges me. "He means you, honey."

I look over at a man wearing a three-piece suit and a wide smile. I'm sure that one look at my face will change his mind about asking me to help him, but other than a slight slip in his smile, which he quickly recovers, he is completely unfazed.

"How 'bout that cookie?"

I use one of the papers (which I've been told are simply called cookie papers) to reach into the big jar of gingerbread cookies on the counter. I start to pull out a gingerbread man in a pair of green shorts with matching suspenders when I feel a hand on my arm.

"He'll want a girl," Gina says.

The man grins at me. "The girls are a bigger cookie for the same price." I grab a gingerbread girl with a blue polka-dotted dress and slide it into a bag. I hand it across the counter to the man.

"Grazie," he says before shuffling down the counter to talk with Mary while she takes his money.

Customers continue to trickle in, but the urgency with which they order seems to diminish. A dozen or so people sit at the tables on the sidewalk in front of the diner, reading newspapers, sipping coffee, and munching on pastries. Most of them are older people dressed far too warmly for the sun, which is already hot enough to make the streets steam. But one head stands out from the gray hair and wool caps of the crowd. I stare at the girl as she folds down the front of her paper and takes a bite of a cinnamon roll. She has her hair pulled back in a ponytail, which isn't unusual, but the color makes her stand out. Her hair is blue. Startlingly blue. Even bluer when the sun hits it. Not sky blue or navy blue, but *blue* blue–blueberry blue.

"Cute boy?" Gina asks, looking out at the tables in the front. I start to shake my head, but Gina's eyes go big. She's already around the counter and to the front door before I have a chance to say anything. She yanks the door open and stomps over to the girl with the blue hair. While I can't hear what she's saying, I can see *how* she's saying it. The blue-haired girl rolls her eyes, making Gina's face go nearly purple. Now I can make out some of the words. *Late* and *disrespectful* filter in toward us. Everyone at the tables has stopped to watch the show.

"Mom," the girl says, her voice carrying through the open door. "Chillax." Gina looks like her head is about to pop off.

Grace snorts and Mary just looks worried, which I've gathered is her normal state. Nonna comes out of the back at that moment, wiping her hands on her apron. When she sees what's happening out front, she hustles to the door even faster than Gina did. Once outside, Nonna begins yelling at Gina, her arms waving. Soon both women's arms are waving so much they look like the loons on our lake just before they jump into the air and fly away. The girl with the blue hair leans back and takes a drink of her coffee, clearly enjoying the show. Gina finally comes back in, quiet but still simmering. Nonna bends and says something to the girl, who folds her paper under her arm, picks up her cup and plate, and follows Nonna inside.

The distraction gives me a chance to duck back into the kitchen. It's one thing to meet dozens of strangers across a glass pastry case, but it's another to see someone my own age up close. When I enter, there's a scale, a stack of parchment squares, and a huge mound of cookie dough on one of the marble counters in the kitchen. Within moments Nonna joins me, followed by the blue-haired girl. I duck my head, hoping the girl won't look my way.

"Measure out one-pound portions," Nonna says, handing me a pair of plastic gloves. "Logs, wrap, freezer."

I stare at the mountain of dough and start carving hunks off it with a scraper. I'm surrounded by one-pound islands of cookie dough when someone joins me at the counter. A glint of blue makes me close my eyes.

"Hey," the girl says.

"Hey," I mumble. I had mostly forgotten what I looked like while it was slamming out front, but in the too-hot kitchen, in close proximity to a girl my age, I am very aware of how my face must look to her. I wish she had chosen to stand on the left side of me, the normal side. But if she notices me at all, she doesn't let on. She just starts rolling the mounds of dough into fat snakes and then wrapping them in squares of parchment. By the time we finish, Nonna delivers another mountain of dough to us.

"I hate peanut butter," the girl says, nodding at the new mound. I glance over at her, but she keeps rolling out the cookie dough snakes. "I mean, not hate like I hate war or people who don't recycle or my mother. It's more like a strong aversion." I glance at her again. She's smiling. "Okay, I don't *hate* my mother." She sighs. "That makes me sound like a psychopath. My mom's just sometimes so—" She doesn't finish, but I nod anyway.

The girl looks at me. "Yours too?" she asks.

"Yeah," I say, thinking of the last year. The girl stops rolling and turns toward me.

"I'm Fig," she says, holding out her gloved hand. I lift my face and look at her full on for the first time, expecting her to drop her hand or at least flinch, but she doesn't. She just beams at me. "In Western culture, it's common practice to shake hands when you meet someone," Fig says, her hand still held out between us. I take her hand. "And now you tell me your name," she prompts.

"Mia," I say.

"Good to meet you, Mia," she says, giving my hand a firm shake. She turns back to the dough and begins grumbling about the stench of peanuts. "So . . ." Fig looks at me and tilts her head. "Who's punishing you?"

I stiffen. "What do you mean?" I don't bother to keep the defensiveness out of my voice, and brace myself for the punch line.

"Well, obviously, you must have made someone mad. Otherwise, why would you be sentenced to a summer working here?" She waves her hand around the kitchen.

I don't know how to answer, but I manage some kind of noncommittal shrug.

"Fine," she says. "Keep your secrets. I won't tell you mine either."

I frown down at my hands. *Good job, Mia. You just alienated the one person your age who has actually been human to you in the last year.* But then Fig starts laughing.

"Okay. I don't have any secrets." She drops her voice

to a whisper. "Not like I haven't tried, but with my family, it's completely impossible." She smiles at me again. "They're everywhere." She makes her voice all wobbly and spooky. I catch myself grinning and then even laughing, something I haven't done in a long time.

Nonna comes back with another batch of dough. This time it's brown and smells like Christmas. "I knew you two would be friends," she says. Fig rolls her eyes, but her face is pure happy. "Fiona," Nonna says over her shoulder. "We need more cannoli cream."

"Fiona?" I ask once Nonna is out of earshot. "I thought you said your name was Fig."

"Nonna's the only one who calls me that. Everyone else calls me Fig." She looks at me and sighs. "Fiona Imogene Greico." She traces her initials in the flour on the counter. *FIG.* "It's better than what they used to call me." She drops her voice to a whisper. "Fatty." Fig lifts one eyebrow as if challenging me to disagree. Then she slaps her hand against her forehead, leaving a floury mark right over her left eye. "Man, that was my one secret." She sighs. "Okay, now I got nothing."

We spend the rest of the morning mixing icings and fillings and cutting up fruit. Fig grumbles whenever her mother comes into the kitchen, but she's not very convincing, because as soon as her mother is gone, she's laughing again. The door from the front into the kitchen keeps spitting out relatives every few minutes. All the names make my head spin.

"I don't know how I'm ever going to remember everyone's name," I say.

"Don't worry," Fig says after I meet *another* cousin. "I
can't even keep them all straight."

Finally, Nonna tells us we're finished and hands us
paper lunch bags, instructing us to grab drinks from the
cooler out front.

"Come on," Fig says. She leads me past her mother and
her aunts, who press cookies into our hands, and around
the counter to the front of the deli, where the tables are
starting to fill up with people coming in for lunch. We stop
at the cooler and Fig grabs a couple of bottles of ginger ale
for us.

"Let's sit outside," she says. "Away from the prying eyes."
We both look over at her various family members manning the counter, wiping down tables and yelling orders to
other family members running the grill. Several of them
are watching us. "See?" she says. "And they wonder why I'm
always taking off."

Fig leads me out onto the sidewalk and toward the table
she was sitting at when I first saw her. A woman trips over
a crack in the sidewalk because she's more intent on staring
at me than looking where she's going. My cheeks burn. Fig
looks at me for a moment.

"Don't worry," she says. "I get that all the time." She
yanks her hair out of her ponytail and it spills down over
her shoulders in a blue waterfall. "You'll just have to get
used to it if you hang out with me."

I simply look at her. She cannot be serious. I'm 99 percent sure that *she* was not the one who almost caused the woman to turn her ankle.

Fig takes a bite of her pickle. "You should have seen it when I had my hair zebra striped. It was awesome."

I shake my head at her, and feel my cheeks going back to normal. Fig keeps looking at me while I unwrap my sandwich. I take a bite of it, chew, and swallow.

"How long have you been working here?" I ask.

"A couple of months." I am surprised, but she doesn't elaborate. I expected her to say *forever*. We sit there, munching on our sandwiches and sneaking bits of each other's cookies. Then Fig starts telling me stories. She calls them "The File of Crazy Tales from the Brunelli Family." Somewhere in the middle of all her talking, I realize I'm with someone who's not looking at me like I'm a monster, or who *isn't* looking at me because I'm a reminder. Then my phone buzzes where it's resting on the table.

I pick up my phone and look at the screen. *Mom*. Three letters are all it takes to yank me back and remind me that I'm not supposed to smile or laugh. I'm not supposed to forget. Truth is, I'm not really even supposed to be alive.

Chapter Four

I shouldn't have answered the phone. Fig tries to give me privacy, but that's pretty hard to do when you're only a table-length apart. Finally she stands, collects our empty lunch bags and bottles, and makes a gesture toward the trash can near the entrance to Brunelli's. I nod, watching her bright blue hair catch the sunlight as she walks away.

"Hi, Mom," I say.

"How are you?" she asks, but she doesn't really want to know, because she immediately launches into a long explanation about how the weather is in Napa and how they put a hold on all fruitcake production until the citron issue is resolved. I interject the appropriate *um-hum*s and *really*s.

"I've been trying to reach your father," she says, finally

getting to the reason she called. "You don't know where he is. Do you?"

"Somewhere on the Gulf Coast," I say. She's silent for a long moment, and I think maybe she was going to ask where I am or how I like New York, but she doesn't.

I hear voices in the background and then my mother's voice speaking to them. "Listen," she says to me. "It's going to be a while before I can talk to you again."

"Why?" I ask.

She's silent for several moments. "I need to go," she says at last. I stare at the tabletop, wishing she would say something more. Something to explain or defend or anything. But all she does is repeat that she won't be able to talk to me for a while. She doesn't give me a chance to ask any questions. She eventually tells me she loves me, which might have been nice, except she doesn't actually say "I love you," but "Love ya." The fact that she can't even say those three words really says it all. My mother used to tell us she loved us about seventeen times a day, with words and notes in our lunches, a triple squeeze of our hands, and heart-shaped pancakes on cold winter mornings. Now, she can't even manage it once in more than ten months.

"I'm going to go," she says.

"Okay," I say. "Bye." But she's already gone.

I can feel the questions radiating from Fig when I go inside, but something in my eyes makes her keep her distance. Nonna's hug of thanks threatens to unglue me as I confirm that no, they didn't scare me off and yes, I'll be back in the morning.

The five-minute walk back to Veronica's feels like five years. I pull out the keys Veronica left for me and let myself in. If she asks me any questions, my excuse is ready. *I'm very tired. I think I'm going to go lie down.*

"Hello?" I say softly, then again, a little louder. My voice echoes back at me. There's no one home. I climb into my bed, and notice I smell of sugar and vanilla and pickles. I stare at the ceiling. I was so busy all morning that I barely had time to think about anything other than what was going on right then. But now, alone, everything comes pouring back in. I force my thoughts away from Maine and my father's goodbye. I tell myself not to think of my mother. Because I doubt very much she's thinking of me.

After an hour of staring at the barbed wire cross hung above my bed, I hear the front door. Hard heels on the parquet. The door shutting. The locks. One, two, three. More click-clacking and then the clink of keys on the marble table in the hall.

Veronica clears her throat. It's the lamest fake cough I've ever heard. The *hem-hem*s get louder. I get up, walk to the door, and pull it open. "I see you're up," she says.

"I'm up," I say. She looks past me, to the bed, and then up at the ceiling where the cross hangs.

"Your mother made that," she says. I stop and look back at her. "I thought you might—" She stops midsentence, lost in thought. I wait, but she doesn't continue. I walk past her toward the bathroom, where I'm careful not to look in the mirror. Veronica follows me in and watches as I turn on the water in the sink, and hold my fingers under it while it warms up. I splash water on my face and reach for the bottle of soap on the back of the counter. It's not the same one that was here earlier. I peer at it with one eye as I squirt a blob of it into my palm. I lift it to my face, but immediately pull my hands away. "What is this?" I ask, squinting at my grandmother through the water dripping into my eyes.

"I picked it up this morning," she says. "It's to even out your skin." I glare at the purplish goo coating my hands. It smells like strawberries that have been left out on the counter too long. I hold my breath and rub the goo all over my face as quickly as I can, then rinse it all off before I take another breath. I grope for a towel on the rack behind me. Once my face is dry, I turn toward her.

"Better," she says. "Look." She points at the mirror.

"I'll take your word for it." I haven't intentionally looked at myself since I dropped the mirror in the hospital, shattering it into dozens of pieces. I don't intend to start now.

"I spoke with Mrs. Brunelli." I look over at her. "She said you were a very nice girl." I nod. "She also said I was very lucky to have you as a granddaughter." She turns and walks out of the bathroom. This is where most grandmothers would hug their grandchildren and tell them that they *know* how lucky they are. For Veronica, it seems like the revelation came as a surprise.

I walk down the hall, following the scent of lavender

that seems to trail behind Veronica wherever she goes. She walks to the chair by the window and sits, pulling a book onto her lap. I look at her for a moment, wondering if I should say something. She slides a pair of reading glasses from the table beside her and then looks at me.

"Mia, I'm not going to hover," she says. "I expect you to use good judgement and make good choices." She sounds scripted and forced, like she's repeating lines from a play. "I know teenage girls need a little room." She presses her lips together as if she'd like to say more, but won't allow herself to. "You should explore a little. Take your phone. Be back before dark."

"What about church?" I ask tentatively, afraid of the answer.

"I only expect you to accompany me on Sundays," she says, and I nearly sigh with relief. "It's a lovely day out," she says, opening the book. "You should go for a walk."

From her tone, I can tell this is not a suggestion, even though I have no idea where I'll go. I head back to my room and take my bag from the hook on the door. Keys. Phone. Money. I glance at the subway pass Veronica left for me, and take it just in case. I'm halfway out the door before I return and grab my camera for safe keeping.

Veronica has turned her chair more toward the window to catch the sunlight. "I guess I'll—" I begin. Veronica raises her hand and half waves at me.

"Enjoy," she says. "Just be back by dark." I practice her wave all the way down in the elevator. It's something between a royal wave and a dismissive one. I wave

Veronica-style at the doorman on the way out. He stares at me and shakes his head.

The sunlight is so bright when I step outside that it makes my eyes water. I start down the sidewalk, pausing at some of the card tables set up along the curb like an impromptu flea market. One vendor selling handcrafted earrings has half a dozen mirrors arranged around her wares. I catch a glimpse of my red hair as I pass.

Two men stand arguing over a broken crate of cabbages. A man in a tuxedo walks past me, trailing dozens of pink and white balloons. I press my back against a wall to let people around me, feeling overwhelmed by it all. It's so loud and bright and busy. And everyone seems to be in a hurry to get somewhere.

A line of children all holding on to a rope pass by.

"Stay in line," their teacher calls. "Anyone caught not holding the rope will be spending their park time on the bench." I decide to follow them, thinking maybe a park will be less hectic.

A man stands on a literal soapbox at the entrance to the park. A sandwich board warns passersby of *The End!!!* "You there," he yells, pointing at me. "Judgment is coming!" I hurry past his accusing finger.

My phone vibrates, and I pull it free from my pocket. I have three missed calls, and all are from the same number, a local one but not one I recognize. There's also a text.

Call me! Fig.

While I stand there debating whether I should call her or not, my phone rings. It's Fig again.

"Finally!" she says before I can even say hello. "Where are you?"

"Um—" I hesitate, watching a woman with purple feet arranging crystals on a table in front of her.

"Meet me at West Fifty-Third in twenty," she says.

"Where is—"

"Just walk to Fourth Street station and get on the M."

"Fourth, then M," I repeat, hoping I can figure out what that means.

"Hurry," Fig says. She hangs up before I can respond.

I pull the subway pass out of my bag and look at it. This should be interesting, given I've never ridden a subway before. I think about calling Fig back and telling her . . . what? That I'm busy? I've never been a good liar. Besides, the thought of going back to Veronica's makes me feel claustrophobic. I look up at the street sign on the corner, then check the map app on my phone. If I'm going to meet Fig in twenty minutes, I'm going to have to hurry.

The subway ends up being better and worse than I imagined. As I'm waiting on the platform, I decide every nasty smell in the universe drifts down into the tunnels and then stays. I freak out the whole time I'm down ther—I blame my father and his jokes about people getting lost underground and being found by Mole People. But I don't see any Mole People, just a lot of regular people. The stops are easy to figure out, and in no time I'm climbing the stairs back up to the street.

The sunlight blinds me again as I walk up the stairs from the subway. The buildings are much taller here and people seem even more impatient to get where they're going. I spot Fig when my eyes adjust to the light. She's changed from the clothes she was wearing at the diner. Now she's wearing a man's suit vest over a tie-dyed T-shirt. Her lower half is covered in blue leggings and—

"Is that a ballerina tutu?" I ask, walking up to her.

She nods and smiles. "Awesome, right? I got it for a buck!" She's carrying a big green duffle bag over one shoulder, and another one rests on the ground at her feet.

"What's all that?" I ask. I nudge the duffle on the ground with the toe of my shoe.

"You'll see," she says. "Come on, we're going to be late."

"For what?" I ask, but she's already walking away from me. And from the duffle on the sidewalk.

"Can you get that?" she yells over her shoulder. I pick up the bag, expecting it to weigh a ton, but it's surprisingly light. I follow Fig as she steps off the curb and begins making her way across the intersection. On the other side, she stops and buys a pretzel from the street vendor. She rips it apart and hands half to me; it's warm in my hand. We stand at the corner, nibbling on our pretzels while we wait for the light to change.

"Where are we going?" I ask.

"You'll see," Fig says. A woman with a triple stroller pushes past, separating me from Fig. A crowd surges around me, and for several moments I think I've lost her, until I see her blue hair, bright in the sunlight just ahead of me. She stops, making several people step quickly to the side to avoid knocking into her. "Come on," she says, pulling at the sleeve of my shirt. We turn at the corner and walk half a block until she stops and faces out into the street. I turn and look.

"MoMA?" I've been to the Museum of Modern Art before. It's awesome for sure, but not really the big secret place I was imagining.

Fig shakes her head impatiently and points at the sidewalk in front of the museum. A cluster of kids about our age are standing, bent over at the waist with their hands on their knees, staring at the pavement. One of them spots us and waves. Fig waves back and yanks my sleeve again, pulling me off the curb and into the street. A cab has to swerve to avoid hitting us.

"Maybe we should use the crosswalk?" I yell over the blaring of horns.

Fig just pulls me harder, and we finally reach the other side. She doesn't let go of my sleeve until she's dragged me up to the trio still staring at the sidewalk. We drop our duffles and step toward them. They shift to one side to give us room. Fig bends over and stares at the sidewalk, and as soon as I look down, I know why.

Two years ago, I came here on a field trip. Most of the kids spent the train ride complaining about the lameness of spending all day staring at a bunch of paintings and sculptures done by people who'd been dead *forever*. I was actually looking forward to seeing the special exhibit, but I didn't say anything. I followed along behind the crowd until we entered the special collection gallery. Right there, separated from me by a velvet rope and about five feet, was a Van Gogh—and not just any Van Gogh, but *Starry Night*. Of course, I'd seen photos of it before. I mean, it's probably one of the most famous paintings in the history of art. But seeing it right there in front of me made me stop walking, stop talking, almost stop breathing.

I just kept standing there, even while everyone else was walking around the gallery, following the droning voice of the docent leading our tour. I kept standing there even when Rachel waved her hand in front of my face and told me she was going to go to the gift shop. Mr. Frank finally came and got me because it was time to leave. The whole time I had the insane urge to reach out and touch the painting, to run my finger along the swirls of color wheeling across the sky. I tried to imagine what it must be like to see the world like that—so beautiful. I tried to talk to Rachel about it, but she just rolled her eyes at me said, "Mia, he was nuts. The guy cut off his own ear."

And here I am staring down at the sidewalk, and *Starry Night* is staring right back up at me. But bigger, way bigger, so that each star is about the size of a bicycle wheel. Though the more I look at it, I realize it's not really *Starry Night* but rather something that hints at it. Something wild and beautiful at the same time. Something like a dream you want to remember, but which only slips away from you the more you think about it. And I have the same urge to touch it even though it's chalk, not oil paint. Even though it's not hung on a wall in a famous museum, just drawn across the sidewalk in the middle of the city.

"You can touch it," the guy beside me says, as if reading my mind. I realize my hand is already reaching toward the sidewalk. I bend and touch the deep-blue streak closest to me. When I lift my finger, it's covered in indigo chalk.

"This was a good secret, right?" Fig asks from where she's standing on the other side of me. I nod and stand up, so I can see more of the drawing. Then I look at the people standing around me. They are all wearing masks like you see doctors wear.

"The chalk dust is bad," says a girl with a Yankees hat. She pulls her mask off so that it hangs around her neck.

"I used to cough for a week after we did one of these things," a guy with dreadlocks says, removing his mask. He loops his arm around Fig's shoulder, rubbing chalk dust all over her sleeve. She pretends to be mad and push him away, but I can tell the last thing she wants is for him to stop.

"It's amazing," I say, suddenly shy. I tilt my head a little so that my hair spills over my cheek.

The guy with the dreads shakes his head. "We're just workers. Coop's the artist." I look over at the guy he's pointing to, who just shrugs.

"Don't be modest, man," Dreadlock Guy says. "This is your best one yet." Yankees Hat Girl and Fig both nod. I'm nodding too, still staring at the swirling colors at my feet.

"You must be Mia," Dreadlock Guy says. I nod, wondering how they know who I am. I look over at Fig, who smiles at me. "I'm Sebastian, and this is Sarah." He points to the girl with the Yankees hat, who takes it off and swats him.

"I can speak for myself," she says. She turns to me and smiles. "Fig told us she was going to bring you today," Sarah says.

I nod, understanding why they know who I am. There can't be that many girls with half a face in New York City.

"So, is Fig's family driving you nuts yet?" Sarah asks. I just shake my head, making her laugh. Her hair catches the sunlight and turns a burnished gold. A guy walking past is staring at her so intently that he trips on the edge of the sidewalk and almost face plants in the shrubbery. Sarah doesn't even notice.

The artist guy bends and adds another swath of blue to the sidewalk. He stands up and dusts off his hands.

"Done," he says. I look at what he's drawn and it's exactly right. It's like when you eat fresh apple pie and it's so good, and then someone adds a scoop of vanilla ice cream and suddenly you realize that's what it was missing.

"That's Cooper," Sarah says, pointing to the artist.

Cooper looks at her. "I too can speak for myself." His voice is teasing and Sarah laughs. Cooper's eyes crinkle as he looks at her. I glance over at Sebastian, who still has his arm resting on Fig's shoulders. Suddenly I feel like a fifth wheel.

Then Cooper pulls his mask down. "Good to meet you,

Mia," he says to me, but his voice sounds like it's coming from far away, because suddenly I realize why no one seems weird about my face. I smile at Cooper in what I hope is a convincing way, but inside I'm sort of a mess. And if Cooper is smiling at me, I can't tell, because where most people have an upper lip, Cooper has nothing. Well, nearly nothing. His upper lip is fine on the sides, but in the middle it's twisted, pleated, attached all wrong. It leaves a hole through which you can just see his teeth and then his gums, and right above that is his nose. The rest of his face is totally normal, actually more than normal. Except for the big empty space, he's what Rachel would have called *nuclear*.

But as soon as I think it, I feel about three inches tall because I realize I am the biggest hypocrite in the whole world. Here I am with half my face looking like I've smeared strawberry jam all over it, and they're all being perfectly nice to me. And I'm freaking out inside that the totally cute guy, who also happens to be an amazing artist, has the tiniest imperfection.

"This is—" I pause both because I'm still beating myself up for being so shallow and because I want to be sure to say the right thing. I look down at the drawing again. "It's completely amazing," I say.

"It's nothing," Cooper says, but this time he doesn't look at me. And I wonder if I blew it—if I just failed some sort of test. And part of me is mad because, *Hello? Who wouldn't be shocked if they saw someone with only half a mouth?* But the bigger part of me shrinks in on itself because no one seemed shocked by the girl with half a face.

"Mia, don't be fooled by my brother's humility," Sarah says. "He's the real deal. If I had an ounce of Cooper's talent, I'd be strutting around here like I was empress of the universe, but Cooper? He's all, 'It's nothing.'" She does a spot-on impression of his voice. She then groans. "Where is the justice in the world?"

Sebastian rolls his eyes and looks at me. "Don't let *her* fool you—Sarah is an amazing artist. I'm the one who should be depressed. You guys are talented, good-looking, smart—" He trails off, like he's in pain. "What do I have?" His eyes dance with laughter as he's talking, and I see Fig roll her eyes.

"I'm not going to tell you *again* how awesome you are," Fig says.

Sebastian looks at me. "What about you, Mia?" He nods at the camera hanging around my neck. "Are you one of the artist types who will crush my self-esteem too?"

"I, um . . ." I don't know what to say. I'm not really good at anything. Nothing I want to share, at least.

"She makes killer cannolis," Fig says, rescuing me from the awkwardness.

"Seriously?" Sebastian asks, smiling.

"I can make cannolis," I admit, silently thanking Nonna for that new skill.

"And black and whites and rugelach and strudel," Fig says.

"And coffee," I say. "But just regular. Not decaf." This makes everyone laugh, even Cooper.

"What about gingerbread?" Sebastian asks, like it's the most important question in the universe.

"Not yet," I say. Sebastian looks crushed. I think of the never-ending baking list. I'm certain gingerbread was listed there. "By the end of the week, for sure," I say. This makes him grin, his teeth so white against his caramel skin. I steal a glance over at Cooper to see if he's smiling too, but he's looking back down at his drawing again.

Fig clears her throat, making me look at her. The way she's watching me makes me blush, although I can't really say why. It's like she knows what I'm thinking, which makes me a little uneasy.

"Little help?" Fig asks, kicking the duffles at her feet.

Sarah grabs one of them and I grab the other. We follow Fig to the other side of the steps that lead up into the museum. I have to force myself not to look at the fountain. I can remember standing there and throwing in a penny the last time I was here. I have no idea what I wished for. If I'd have known what was going to happen, I would have wished for something else.

Fig directs us to put the duffle bags near the wall of the museum. She bends and unzips one, drawing T-shirts from its depths and dropping them onto the ground. She tosses one to Sarah and starts tugging a large white bundle free from the bag. Sarah pulls one of the T-shirts over her head. ART ATTACK is scrawled across the front in heavy black script.

"What's Art Attack?" I ask.

"Art Attack," Fig says, "is us." She points at herself and Sarah and waves her hand over to Sebastian and Cooper, who are standing off to one side while people look at his drawing and drop coins into an upturned fedora resting on the sidewalk.

Fig begins unrolling the big white bundle, which turns out to be one of those canvas drop cloths that painters use to protect floors when they're working. I have to force down another memory, one of my mother painting over a bright orange wall with white paint.

Next, Fig pulls duct tape out of her bag. She secures two corners of the drop cloth and tosses the tape to Sarah, who secures the corners on her side.

Fig stands up and motions for me to come over. She unzips the other bag, the one she was carrying, and starts pulling out big tubes of paint and a box of wet wipes. "Art Attack is something we started doing a couple of months ago," she explains. "We do spontaneous art." Then she looks at the paint tubes she's holding. "There's a surprisingly large amount of planning that goes into the spontaneous part."

I look over at Cooper and Sebastian, who are starting to pack away their things. "What do you do with the money?" I ask, watching as another person drops a folded bill into the fedora.

"We buy supplies with some, but we donate most of it to the local schools to support their art programs." She smiles at the look on my face. "I know," she says. "We're so altruistic." She laughs when she says it. "Here, I'll trade you."

She reaches for my camera, but I pull back, a little unsure. "Just to keep it safe while we work." I nod and hand it over. She tucks it into the bag, out of sight, and hands me half a dozen tubes of paint and a big roll of paper towels.

Sarah, Fig, and I haul everything over to where we've taped down the giant drop cloth. There's already a crowd gathering. Sarah takes off her Yankees hat and puts it upside down right at the front.

Fig pulls gloves out of her pocket and puts them on. She tosses a pair to me and another to Sarah. "We call this one *All Walks of Life*," she says. "Who's first?" Fig asks the crowd.

Several little kids and one adult raise their hands. I'm surprised, because she doesn't offer any explanation. She picks a small boy who is right in front. "Take your shoes off," she says. He looks at the woman holding his hand. She nods. He immediately drops and pulls off his sneakers and socks, revealing very pale feet that don't match his sun-browned legs.

Sarah brings over a couple of tubes of paint. "Pick one," she says, holding them toward the boy. He thinks for a moment before pointing to the tube of red. Sarah unscrews the top of the tube and instructs the boy to hold his foot still. "It's going to tickle a little."

The boy braces himself, half excited, half nervous. Sarah squirts a big blob of paint into one hand and starts spreading it all over the bottom of his foot. Now I know what the gloves are for. The boy has his eyes shut tight, trying as hard as he can to be still while she finishes that foot and begins working on the other, this time using blue on her other hand.

"Okay," Fig says, coming over and helping him stand up on the tarp. "Walk around." He takes a tentative step forward and then another. He looks back to see his footprint on the tarp, then takes a few more steps, looking back each time. Step. Look. Step. Look. The paint wears off about halfway across the canvas. Fig leads the boy back to his mother, who accepts several wet wipes. The boy is smiling and pointing at his footprints, while his mother attempts to wipe the paint out from between his toes.

"Who's next?" Fig asks.

We spend the next hour painting feet and letting people walk across the canvas. Cooper and Sebastian come over at some point to help us roll out another drop cloth when the first one is full. Mostly kids volunteer, but there are a few brave adults. We discover one of the adults is a curator at the museum. Cooper sits and talks with him while the man cleans off his feet. Every once in a while, a member of ART ATTACK will talk to the gathered crowd and tell them why we're here and what the money is going toward. Sarah says things like *appreciation of the arts* and *creative energy* while Cooper uses words like *the power of expression* and *artistic anarchy*. Fig just tells everyone that the paint smooshing through your toes feels cool.

It isn't until I'm squatting beside a little girl with blonde hair and trying to help her wipe green paint off her foot that anyone says anything about my face. "What happened to you?" the little girl asks, reaching out to touch my cheek. I jerk my face away. No one, other than a few doctors, has touched my face in almost a year. I look down and see the girl's eyes welling up with tears. "I'm sorry," she says, her voice trembling.

"It's okay," I say. She looks at me and I force a smile. "Really. You just surprised me." She nods and tries for a smile herself, but it's small, barely a tenth of the one she had earlier.

"Does it hurt?" she asks softly.

"Sometimes," I say. It's the truth, but not in the way she means. And really, it hurts all the time, just some times more than others. She looks at me for a long moment, then holds out her hand.

"My brother slammed my finger in the door," she says, showing me her finger that's wrapped in a Disney Princesses bandage.

"I'll bet it was an accident," Cooper says from beside me. I didn't even know he was listening. The little girl looks at him for a moment before she nods and smiles. He said the exact right thing. Something I wouldn't even think to say.

"It was," she says. "He'd never do that on purpose." She pulls on her sandals and stands up. I notice that her feet are still slightly green. She runs off to where a woman and a little boy are standing, looking at Cooper's drawing. She's back in a few moments, clutching a ten-dollar bill, which she hands to Cooper. "You're nice," she says before running off again.

Cooper looks my way, and for a second I almost feel like he can see inside of me. And I wonder how I would feel if he really could. Relieved that I didn't have to hide anymore. But also devastated at what he'd think. Then Cooper is up and moving away to help someone else.

We keep working. Every so often, I'll look up and catch Cooper watching me, but mostly it's just paint and wipe and paint and wipe.

"I'm out," Sarah says, holding up a spent tube of paint. The ground around her is littered with empty tubes in all the colors of the rainbow.

"Me too," Fig says, holding up her own flattened tube. They both look at me.

"I have a little," I say, holding up the tube of purple I was using. "Maybe enough for one more."

"Good," Fig says. She turns and faces the crowd that is gathered, still watching us. "Thank you, everyone," she says, loudly. "We're all finished for today." There are a few groans from the crowd. "But look for us around the city," she says. "We'll be where you least expect it."

"In front of an art museum is not exactly where I'd *least* expect to see us," Sebastian says from where he's standing beside me. Fig points at him and pantomimes a zipping motion across her lips. This makes him laugh. "She's got ears like a bat," he tells me.

The crowd starts to filter away as Cooper and Sebastian roll up the first canvas, which has had a chance to dry. Sarah dumps the money from her hat into the backpack.

I swear the sides of it are bulging a little, although that seems hard to believe.

"You," Fig says, pointing at me. "Shoes off."

I hold up one of my still-gloved hands and shake my head. "I don't think I want paint smooshing between my toes." I look around at the others, hoping to find someone to agree with me, but everyone suddenly pretends to be way too busy to jump to my aid. Fig stands there, watching me with one eyebrow raised. I take a breath. "Okay," I say. I sit on the sidewalk and yank off my Chucks and my socks. I squirt a blob of purple on one foot and then the other. It feels cold against the soles of my feet. I smear it around and then stand up on a clean spot on the canvas.

"Move around," Sarah says. I look over at all of them staring at me. *Sure*, now they're paying attention. I take a step forward and then another.

"Boring!" Sebastian says.

"What do you want me to do?" I ask.

"Something interesting," Fig says.

I take a deep breath and close my eyes. I think of Fig's skirt that she bought for a dollar, and then I think of Rachel and me spinning in our yard faster and faster until we'd fall onto the grass laughing. I put my arms over my head and twirl in a circle like a ballerina. I feel foolish and brave in equal measure. Sebastian yells his approval.

Spinning with my eyes closed makes me dizzy. I stop and open my eyes, feeling lightheaded. I look down and realize I'm almost out of paint anyway. When they all clap

for me, I curtsy while holding out an imaginary skirt, figuring I can't possibly make any more of a fool of myself. I
step off the canvas and wipe the paint from my feet. I can't
quite get it all, leaving my toes faintly violet. As I step back
into my socks and shoes, I decide I'm not sure Fig was right
about the smooshy feeling. My feet feel sort of clammy and
yucky. I help clean up, dropping the spent tubes of paint
into the duffle (Fig says you can recycle those) and tossing the wads of wipes and paper towels into the nearby
trash can.

Soon everything but the final canvas is put away.
Sebastian scrawls *Art Attack* and a web address across the
top of the tarp with a thick black marker. The handwriting
matches the writing on their T-shirts.

"Now we just wait," Fig says. She looks up at the
museum.

"The curator who gave us permission to do this is coming back to pick it up. He's going to hang it in the lobby,"
Sarah says.

"Wow," I say. I spot my camera peeking out of the duffle and retrieve it.

"What kind of photographs do you take?" Sarah asks.

"Mostly people," I say. "Faces." I think about the photo
on my camera. The one I never look at. I thought I wanted
to be an artist once, but that was a long time ago. And that
was a different me.

The same curator who was brave enough to walk across
our canvas is walking toward us and smiling. "Good news,"

he says when he reaches us. "The director says we can put up a collection box below the installation." I see Fig grin at the word *installation*.

"Awesome," Fig says. Sebastian and Cooper bump fists and Sarah does a little dance. We all help him roll up the canvas, careful not to smear the paint. Cooper tells Sarah she should head over to Fig's, that he'll meet her after they finish hanging the canvas. Sarah nods and she and Fig each shoulder a bag. Sarah hands my camera back to me.

"Good to meet you, Mia," Sebastian says. Cooper nods slightly, and I'm surprised at how that small gesture makes my heart beat a little faster. Cooper and Sebastian each take an end of the canvas and begin following the curator up the steps.

"Coming, Mia?" Fig calls from behind me.

"Yeah," I say. I start down the sidewalk to where Fig and Sarah are waiting for me. I sneak a look at Cooper, but he and Sebastian have already started walking inside.

I follow Fig and Sarah. We all ride the subway back downtown, talking and laughing about nothing. We take turns carrying the mostly empty bags after we climb out of the subway. We pause at the entrance to Brunelli's. I learned this morning that Fig's whole family lives in the apartments above the restaurant. "Guess I'll see you bright and early," Fig says, making a face.

"Except that it's still dark at four," I say, smiling.

"Just early then," Fig says. Sarah repeats Sebastian's assertion that it was good to meet me. Joey, Fig's uncle, opens the door for Sarah and Fig, making me wonder if he was assigned to watch for their arrival. He gives me a nod before letting the door shut behind them.

The sky is just starting to darken when I reach Veronica's building. I pull out my keys, but I needn't have bothered. The doorman is holding the door wide for me by the time I make it to the top of the steps. "Thank you," I say, wondering if I could ever get used to having someone in my life whose sole purpose was to open the door for me.

I ride up in the elevator with a man who smells strongly of either cheese or feet. He bids me a good night as I step off onto the fourth floor. Veronica left me a note, saying she'll be out late and that I should get to bed early so I'll "be on time for work in the morning." I frown at the note, wondering if that was part of what made my mother crazy. Veronica's implication that I wasn't on time *this* morning peeks out from between the lines of her perfect penmanship.

I take a long shower, letting the cool water wash away big-city grime that seems to cling to everything. I forgo the covered plate of chicken and rice Veronica left in the refrigerator and eat a dinner of apple and peanut butter standing at the sink.

I drop into bed early, not because Veronica told me to but because I'm wiped. Just before I turn out the light, my phone vibrates, announcing an incoming text. I pick it up off the stack of books I'm using for a nightstand. It's from my dad. There aren't any words; just an image attached. I click on it, and it fills the screen.

A single perfect sand dollar rests on wet sand. My dad's Bean boot has snuck into the corner of the shot. That bit makes me smile more than the sand dollar. My dad can't seem to keep himself from spilling into every photo he takes. His thumb. His shadow. A low-hanging fishing lure. I start to respond with a smiley face emoji. Then I remember the ride in the truck and the dozens of silent breakfasts and the endless evenings filled with old movies and too much jazz music. I click my phone off without responding. One photo doesn't mean much stacked against all of that.

I feel anger welling up in me again and try to tamp it down. I am not allowed that emotion. Sadness, grief, regret, and despair are all available to me, but my mother's departure followed soon after by my father's announcement that he was going to take the summer to re-up his rescue diver certification made it clear that whatever kindness I am offered is more than I deserve.

I replace my phone on my makeshift bedside table. I think for once I might actually have a good night's sleep, but I don't. I have the same dream I always have. But this time instead of just sound, there's Rachel. A still shot of her, like a photograph. Then there's the sound of squealing tires and glass breaking and the sound of screaming. And then it's silent.

Chapter Five

The alarm on my phone starts beeping at 3:30. I push myself up to sitting and rub at my eyes. I dress, brush my teeth, pull on my shoes, all with the lights off. When I finish, the door to Veronica's room is still closed. I raise my hand to knock and say goodbye, but stop before my knuckles hit the door. Somehow, instead of commiseration about the early hour or even a simple *have a good day,* an interaction with her would likely mean more scrutiny, more suggestions for how I might improve myself.

I hurry down the stairs and outside. Brunelli's is only two blocks away from my grandmother's apartment. The city is almost quiet this early in the morning. Even the cabs seemed hushed as they slide by. A truck, with its bed filled with roses, rolls past. The smell is like the cliffs above

Farseer Cove in Maine, where Rachel and I used to pick rosehips to make tea that neither of us would ever drink.

I hurry across the street. I can see Brunelli's glowing sign from the corner. It alternates between reading "Hot Soup" and "Air-Conditioned." Joey opens the door at my knock, smiling and bobbing his head to whatever is coming out of the earbuds that seem permanently stuck in his ears.

"Morning!" he says way too loudly.

I start to respond, but he's already turned his back to me so he can lock the door. Nonna comes out of the back, her glasses perched on the end of her nose. She smiles when she sees me, but keeps talking into the phone she has wedged between her ear and her shoulder.

"You're killing me here," she says as she walks past. She looks at the clipboard in her hand. "Three dollars a pound!" Nonna listens for a moment. "You'll be sorry that you weren't kinder to me when I'm dead." Nonna winks at me.

"She always tells them that," Fig says, sliding up beside me.

"Two twenty," Nonna says. She listens, and the sides of her mouth inch upward. Apparently, she got her price.

"And they always fall for it," Fig says, shaking her head. "Come on." I follow her into the kitchen. Fig pulls open the door of one of the refrigerators and rummages inside for a moment before extracting a carton of orange juice. She pulls two mugs down from the hooks that hang from the underside of all the cabinets and pours juice into both of them. She slides one toward me and lifts the other.

"Cheers," she says. She tips the mug to her mouth and takes a long drink. "So," she says, wiping her mouth with the back of her hand. "After work, I want you to come somewhere with me."

"Where?" I ask.

"It's a secret."

"Another one?" This girl is full of secrets, whether or not she keeps them.

She grins and then takes another drink before lowering the mug to look at me across its rim. "And nothing you can say will pry it from me."

Nonna comes back into the kitchen, slapping the clipboard against her leg and smiling. "Guess what Saturday is."

Fig shrugs. "No idea." Nonna swats her arm lightly with the clipboard. Fig tilts her head to the side, as if thinking. "Arbor Day?" I can tell she knows what Saturday is, but she's enjoying teasing Nonna.

"Fiona, you know that Saturday is one of the most important days of the year."

I can think of only a handful of important holidays in June, but none of them are this weekend. She's got me stumped.

Fig laughs. "Is it maybe—" She pauses, making Nonna swat her again. "Cannoli Day?"

"Yes!" Nonna says, grinning. "So, which of you is going to—"

Fig puts her finger on her nose. "Not it!" She looks at me. I narrow my eyes at her, but she just keeps tapping her nose, like that lets her off the hook. "Sorry," she says.

"Sorry about what?" I ask, starting to worry a little.

Nonna grabs my hand and pulls me toward the hall that leads to her office.

"Wait here," she says, depositing me outside her office. She disappears down the hall, but returns in a moment with a big brown-and-white bundle wrapped in plastic, which she hands to me. I take it in both arms, noting there is a hanger in the midst of it. I carry it back into the kitchen, where Fig is standing, trying desperately not to laugh.

"What is this?" I ask, holding the hanger and watching as the plastic bag unfurls toward the floor.

Grace pushes into the kitchen with her hands full of the empty pastry baskets. She takes one look at what I'm holding and starts laughing. She doesn't even bother trying to hide it. Mary pokes her head in to see what the noise is about. In only a few moments, the kitchen is filled with half a dozen Brunellis, the dairy guy, and the produce woman. And they're all looking at me.

"Try it on!" Grace says.

That's when I realize I'm holding a costume.

"Um, I don't think—" I say, holding the bag as far away from myself as I can. Fig walks over, lifts the plastic, and removes the costume from its hanger.

"It's not that bad," Fig says, but her voice isn't that convincing. She wrinkles her nose. "Okay, it is pretty bad, but at least you're totally covered. No one will know it's you."

"What is it?" I ask, still unable to figure out anything from the mound of fabric that Fig's holding in her arms.

"It's a cannoli," Fig says, like the answer is obvious.

"A cannoli?" I repeat. This makes everyone in the kitchen start laughing again. Fig shoots them a dirty look, but this only makes them laugh harder.

"You might as well try it on," Fig says. "They won't stop until you do."

"I'm pretty sure seeing me dressed up as a giant Italian pastry isn't going to make the laughing stop," I say, but Fig has already unzipped the costume and is holding it open for me to step into it.

I let her help me zip it up and then accept the head-piece, which is a large poof of white fabric. I place it on my head and lower the front flap down, noting that I can still see out of the thin fabric. As expected, seeing me dressed up does not make the rest of the staff stop laughing. I feel my cheeks heat up, but then Joey walks over and claps me on the back.

"Welcome to the family," he says over the screeching gui-tar riff spitting out of his earbuds. One by one, everyone comes over to welcome me. Grace is the last person to walk over.

"It's official," she says. "Once you don the costume, you become an honorary Brunelli." She gives my shoulder a hard whack before leaving the kitchen. I pull off the head-piece and look at Fig.

"Once a Brunelli, always a Brunelli," she says. She makes her eyes go big. "The only way out now is if you die." This makes me smile, but inside I'm thinking, *If I have to wear this thing in public, I might just die of embarrassment.*

After work, I hurry back to Veronica's apartment to clean up a little. The apartment is empty, making me curious about what Veronica does all day. I leave a note for her before heading back to meet Fig at the restaurant. I write that I'll be back before dark, which is as specific as I can be considering Fig won't tell me anything about where we're going.

I stop at a store on the way back to the diner that has tables set up out front, where every kind of cheap touristy junk is featured: Giant foam hands with I ? NY on them. Snow globes with tiny plastic Statue of Liberty figures inside. Bobble heads of Yankees, Giants, and Nets players. A jar full of sticks that claim to be magic wands sits at the back of one of the tables. The guy manning the tables is staring at me, curious.

"What happened to your face?" he asks. I'm surprised at how blunt he is.

"Accident," I say, trying to keep it short.

"Must have been a bad one," he says.

"Yep," I say. *Duh*, I think.

"I got me a scar too," he says, lifting his shirt. In the midst of all the hair fleecing his stomach, there's a thick, red scar.

"Wow," I say because what do you say when a complete stranger whips up his shirt to reveal a ginormous scar bisecting his ginormous stomach?

He grins at me and lowers his shirt. "You want to buy something?"

"What about one of those," I say, gesturing toward the wands. He grabs one, holds it up, and taps it. A shower of ribbons shoots out of the end, making me jump. I pick up one and tap it like he did. A long black snake erupts from the end, making me scream and the man laugh. He explains the color coding on the ends. I decide to buy one of the yellow ones, handing over three dollars. I stuff the wand into my bag.

"The name's Julio," Scar Man says.

"Mia," I reply.

"Be seeing you, Mia," he says because, apparently, we are now friends.

"Thanks," I say, partly because of the wand and partly because he didn't treat me like some exhibit in a traveling freak show. I start back toward Brunelli's, smiling.

The sidewalk is packed with people, mostly women pushing kids in strollers and joggers heading toward the park. A woman pushing a double stroller (one seat occupied by a baby, the other occupied by a Chihuahua in a sparkly pink dress) forces me off the sidewalk and onto the street. A cyclist swears as he has to swerve around me.

"Watch it!" he yells, looking back over his shoulder as he passes. He stares at my face a beat too long. He narrowly misses running into the open door of a produce truck. He shoots a dirty look back at me as if I'm the cause of his near accident.

I duck my head, my good mood vanishing in a flash. How many times is this going to happen? There are so many people in New York, literally *millions* more than were at home. Every time I turn around, someone is staring at my face, and it's getting old—fast. Even before the accident, I definitely wasn't the most self-confident girl in the world. Now? I don't know how much more of this I can take.

Suddenly, spending the afternoon hiding out in Veronica's apartment doesn't sound so bad. I stop in the middle of the sidewalk and make an abrupt 180.

"Yo, Mia!"

Reluctantly, I turn and see Joey walking toward me, his arms filled with boxes.

"Little help?" he asks.

I close my eyes and touch my cheek. *I'll just go help Joey*, I think. *Then I'll leave.*

I take the topmost box from Joey's arms. Inside are easily a hundred wooden dowels. I walk ahead of Joey and hold the door for him. I step in to see Nonna standing on a stool behind the counter trying to hang one end of a banner that reads *Cannolis at Brunelli's* in big, sparkly-gold print. Half a dozen Brunellis surround Nonna, all with their arms out to catch her if she falls and all yelling at her to get off the stool. Joey places his boxes on a table and walks over to where they are all standing.

"Good God, Mother—" Grace says.

Nonna fixes her eyes on her. "Watch your language," she says. She looks back at the nail just out of her reach. "If I could just—" She lunges upward to hook the end of the banner. She manages to hit the nail, but throws herself off balance in the process. She tips sideways, and Joey catches her before she falls too far.

I notice Fig standing off to one side, unfolding a piece of paper. She's reading it so intently that she hasn't noticed I'm back. I decide that with everyone distracted, I can slip out, but I'm not fast enough.

"Mia!" Grace says. "Dowels. Kitchen. Now." She's not one to waste words. I head for the kitchen, outside of which Grace is making a hurry-up motion with her hand.

Fig is still reading when I walk past her. "Hey," I say. She jumps and presses the sheet of paper against her chest. Her cheeks flush as she folds the paper and stuffs it into the front pocket of her jeans.

"What's up?" she says, trying for casual, but her voice sounds strained, and I can't help but wonder what she was just looking at.

"Mia!" Grace says even louder than before.

Fig smirks at me. I have to walk past Grace to enter the kitchen. She says something under her breath that I don't quite catch. Fig follows me into the kitchen.

"What's that?" Fig asks, pointing to the magic wand that's sticking out of my bag. I put the box of dowels on the island, then hand her the wand. She tilts her head at me, one eyebrow raised. "Is it real?"

"Try it," I say. While she's looking more closely, I pull my camera out of my bag. I hide it behind my back and turn it on as I instruct her on how to use the wand.

She taps it once on the counter and points it straight in

the air. As she lifts her arm, I hold out my camera, adjusting it so that the whole screen is filled with her face. The chicken shoots out of the end of the wand like it's trying to take flight. I click the shutter once then twice, catching her mid-scream on the first one and laughing in the second. And then I realize what I'm doing, and I feel sick. The last photo I took was almost a year ago, and for the last year, I guess some part of me decided that was the last photo I'd ever take.

"Show me," Fig demands. I look up at Fig slowly. She's grinning at me and trying to angle her way over my shoulder to see the screen. I hold it up and she shrieks. "This is so completely awesome," Fig says. She's grinning like crazy. "Help me," she says. I help her twist the chicken back inside the end of the wand. "Come on," she says. "I have to find my mother." I start to put my camera back onto the shelf, but then Fig turns. "Bring it," she says.

Gina is in the cooler in the back, sorting through huge wheels of cheese and big slabs of roast beef. Just seeing the big hunks of meat makes me consider going vegetarian. Somehow when the meat is sliced, you can forget that it was once an animal's leg, but the meat in the cooler clearly looks like animal parts with the skin off. Yuck.

"Mom," Fig says. "Look what Mia gave me." Gina takes the wand from her, and Fig tells her how to work it. Then, behind her mother's back, she makes her eyes go big and pretends to hold up an invisible camera.

I nod, watching for the right moment. When the chicken

springs free from the wand, Gina lets out a blood-curdling scream. I'm so startled, I almost drop my camera, but I manage to get a shot of Gina's face before it goes totally purple and before the cooler starts filling with more of the family, wanting to find out what the latest drama is all about.

"Fiona Imogene Greico!" Gina begins, making a grab for Fig, but Fig's too fast for her. She's already darted out of the cooler and behind one of her uncles. Gina lunges at me next, trying to grab my camera. I scramble back, almost tripping on a jar of pickles on the way out. Gina starts yelling and waving her arms around. Unfortunately, she's still holding the wand with the rubber chicken hanging out of it. The flopping chicken and her incoherent words only make us laugh harder. Gina yells at Joey to do something. Joey shrugs, but turns to Fig and me.

"That wasn't nice, girls," he says. It's good that his back is to his sister, because he's having a hard time keeping a straight face.

"Tell them they could have given me a heart attack," Gina says.

"You could have given her a heart attack," Joey repeats dutifully. We both apologize. Gina glares at us for a long moment, her arms crossed, but then she's smiling and shaking her head, clear she was only fake angry. She nods toward the front. We walk out of the kitchen, followed by Joey. The door swishes closed behind us, cutting us off from the kitchen.

"Nice one," Joey says, high-fiving first Fig then me.

"I heard that!" Gina yells.

"We better get out of here," Fig says. She grabs two gingerbread women for us and we slip outside.

I follow right behind Fig, who is walking really fast. I have to hurry to keep up with her. She stops at the curb and leans against the street post, laughing.

"That was the best," she says, handing me one of the cookies. Fig waves her hand in the direction of the diner. "Big families like mine are all about the noise and drama," she says. She nibbles on one of the arms of the gingerbread woman, frowning as she chews. "Well, mostly," she says, softly. She bites the cookie again, this time taking the whole arm. Then she looks at the cookie. "It's kind of creepy," she says.

"What?" I ask, surprised at how serious her voice is.

"Gingerbread cookies," she says. "I mean, look—" She holds out her armless cookie and shrugs.

"I guess," I say, looking at the uneaten cookie in my hand. Fig is quiet for another moment, and then she shakes her head as if she's trying to get rid of something. She smiles at me, but her smile is a little thin, like she's trying to stretch it too far and it's not quite big enough to fit.

"Let's see the pictures," she says, motioning to my camera. I turn the camera back on and push the play button. I click the back button exactly three times until the first photo I took of Fig, the frightened one, fills the screen. I hand the camera to her and she laughs. She clicks forward once. Then again.

"This one is *awesome*," she says, tilting the camera so that I can see that she's looking at the one I took of Gina. She tilts it back to look at it again, fooling around with the zoom so that her mother's mouth is big enough to fill the screen. "You can almost see her tonsils," she says. "You have to send this to me."

I nod. Fig clicks the camera's back button too many times and I reach out for it, but I'm not fast enough. Fig stares at the photo that I know is there. The only picture I had saved on my camera. Then she looks up at me. I see the one thing I hate in her eyes: pity. She doesn't resist when I take the camera back from her. I click the off button and tuck my camera back into my bag. I fight the urge to touch my face.

"Is that from before?" Fig asks. I look up at her, angry, trying to embarrass her into silence. "I mean, before you . . ." She looks at the right side of my face, the ruined side.

I turn my face away from her. Maybe if I don't say anything, she'll stop.

"Mia—" Fig begins. I know she wants to make me feel better, to tell me it's not that bad. I know she wants to say what everyone says, that I don't look that different. But I don't want her to say any of those things. They are all a lie. Besides, it's not even me in the picture. I should know. I'm the one who took it.

"That's my sister." I can barely breathe as I say it. I pray she heard me over the city noise. I don't want to have to repeat myself.

"She's pretty," Fig says. I close my eyes and force myself to breathe. "Mia—" she says.

"She's dead," I say.

Her chin snaps up and her eyes get huge. She opens her mouth to say something and then shuts it again.

"Where are we going?" I say, cutting off the inevitable *I'm sorry* or *When?* or worse: *How?* I know my voice sounds angry, but I'm not. Not really. I just don't want to talk about it. I look over at Fig, daring her to say anything else, but she doesn't. She just slips her hand into her pocket, touching the paper she has folded there.

"It's a secret," Fig repeats, although I don't know whether she means the paper in her pocket or where she's taking me. Maybe both.

Or maybe she's sort of asking about the photo on my camera, asking if it's a secret too. But it's not. Or if it is, a lot of it is a secret to me too. My psychiatrist told me I'll remember more with time. When I'm ready.

But sometimes I think I don't want to know what really happened that night. It's like the door off our kitchen, the one that leads to our cellar. The one that was always locked. Rachel and I used to tease each other that monsters lived down there. Even when I got older and I knew that it was just where my father stored his guns, the door still scared me. Like there was something else hidden. Something bad.

"Come on," Fig says. She walks toward the curb, tossing her partially eaten cookie into the trash can on the way. I drop mine in too. It breaks in half as it lands beside Fig's.

They lie on top of a folded newspaper, almost but not quite holding hands. I follow Fig across the street. I'm grateful for the noises of the city—the cabs and the construction and chatter—which fill the silence between us. I try to focus on the noise, but I can't. All I can think about is the way those two cookies were lying there side by side, broken. Just staring up at the sky.

Chapter Six

Fig tells me we have to walk several blocks to get to her "secret." We travel down narrow streets lined with trees and shops selling everything from old vinyl records to giant papier-mâché pigs with wings. Fig pulls me into a shop named Deux Gros Nez. A sign inside claims that they have everything a discerning shopper with a prodigious proboscis would want. Shelves are filled with snoot boots (like earmuffs, but for your nose), heavy-duty handkerchiefs, and imported smelling salts. I know Fig brought me here to cheer me up or distract me or just to give me some time, but I find myself falling for it—for her weirdness and her laughter and the way she seems to brighten everything around her. We try on some sunglasses with attached rubber noses—*for your small-nosed friends*, the packaging reads. Fig decides to buy a pair and insists on wearing them back out onto the street.

Another few blocks and we leave funky and enter swanky. Huge skyscrapers replace the brownstones and briefcases, and power suits replace beaded purses and torn jeans. It's so different from Maine, where the trees seem to outnumber the people a billion to one. And where if you go for an early run, you better wear a bell. You don't want to surprise a bear on his morning walk.

"It's just up here," Fig says, leading me around the corner. The last thing I expect to see is Sebastian hanging nearly upside down from what looks like a rock climbing harness. He's hooked to a rope looped over a pole that sticks straight out from a big brick building. All of the other poles along the building are hung with banners advertising *New Lending Rates* and *Zero Interest Financing*. Sebastian is yelling at whoever is holding the other end of his rope, telling him to keep still. I can't see who it is because of the wall of people, but whoever it is, they're laughing like crazy and letting Sebastian flop up and down like a fish on a hook. His dreadlocks are flying in a million different directions, making him look like a wild mop.

I can't believe no one has come and kicked them out or arrested them or something. Then I see a sign they have tacked up on a sandwich board in front of them on the sidewalk. It advertises Art Attack and has the website. Below that is a city permit that apparently gives them the right to hang upside down from a rope fifteen feet in the air. Two policemen are even standing astride their mountain bikes and watching the show.

"And now," Sebastian announces, "I will eat soup upside down." A girl hands a carton of soup and a spoon up to him.

When she turns, I see it's Sarah. She sees us (or more likely sees Fig's hair) and waves. We both wave back. I watch, amazed, as Sebastian manages to eat almost the whole container of soup without spilling any.

"I can't even manage that right side up," Fig says to me. The fake nose bounces up and down on her face as she talks.

"Ta-da!" Sebastian yells, holding the container upside down to prove that it's empty.

Everyone claps. Fig puts her thumb and finger in her mouth and gives a shrill whistle. I aim my camera up at him and zoom in as much as I can, trying to get just his face. He's spinning a little, so I have to time it just right. It's still uncomfortable using my camera again, but I can feel something begin to glow inside of me. It's just a tiny ember like the first spark of a campfire, but it feels good. Sebastian goes on to eat an ice cream cone and to attempt to break the world record for blowing a bubble gum bubble. I watch as he puts no fewer than ten pieces of gum in his mouth and chews. He seems well on his way toward some kind of record, but an overly aggressive blow sends his huge wad of gum shooting out of his mouth and toward the crowd, where it narrowly misses hitting a man in a dark blue business suit. The man just raises an eyebrow and smiles a little.

I can see Sebastian wince, but clearly he's a pro, because he recovers quickly, yelling "Ta-da!" again.

"Is he the cutest or what?" Fig asks. She quickly looks at me. "Do not tell him I said that."

I make a gesture as if locking my lips.

Sebastian is being lowered down to the sidewalk. He manages to hit feet first, which in my book is at least as amazing a trick as any of the others. He talks with the man in the business suit for a moment.

"That's his dad," Fig says. Now that I'm looking for it, I can see the resemblance. Same nose. Same jawline, but that's where the similarities end. Sebastian is all hippie-boho with his dreads and baggy cargo shorts, while his father is a buttoned-up power-suit guy. Sebastian nods at something his father says, and then turns to the crowd still assembled.

"Thank you, everyone. Remember all of your donations are appreciated." He gestures toward the same fedora I saw on the sidewalk at the MoMA. The hat is filled almost all the way to the brim. He unhooks from the rope, which starts disappearing up and over the pole and drops to the ground.

I stand on my tiptoes, hoping to see Cooper holding the other end of the rope. But the guy coiling the rope is short, stocky, blond, and definitely not Cooper. I'm surprised at how disappointed I feel. I glance at Fig, who is smiling at me like she can read my mind. I scowl at her. She makes the same locking motion over her lips, but then starts laughing.

She tucks her new glasses into her pocket and motions for me to follow her, over to where Sebastian is talking to a group of people standing around him.

"I call it artistic eating," he says, waving his hand behind him toward where he was hanging.

As he waves, the sleeve of his shirt rides up, exposing his forearm and a series of round scars that look nearly as ugly as mine. I realize I'm reaching for my own scar as I watch. I quickly drop my hand to my side and tilt my head to make sure my cheek is concealed.

"It's all about taking the ordinary and making it extraordinary," Sebastian says. He winks at Fig, making me think she had something to do with his speech. He unbuckles his harness, pausing to thank people as they drop bills and coins into the hat. Then he steps out of the harness and stows it in a duffle bag. He waves at someone walking back into the building, and I turn and see Sebastian's father disappear inside.

"He came," Fig says to Sebastian.

He nods and shrugs, but I can tell he's really happy. "Stranger things have happened," he says.

Stocky Blond Guy comes over with the rope slung over his shoulder. "Dude, that was awesome. Any time you want me to help, dude, I'm there."

"Thanks for pitching in," Sebastian pauses and makes a face. "Dude." Blond guy doesn't seem to notice the sarcasm in Sebastian's voice.

"Dude, where do you want this?" he asks, lifting the rope.

Sebastian points to the duffle. "Just don't crush the—"
The blond guy heaves the rope onto the bag. The crunching
noise the rope makes when it hits whatever is inside the
bag makes Sebastian wince.

"What, dude?" he asks, turning back around.

"Nothing," Sebastian says. "Thanks again." He endures
a high five, which he takes almost as well as all the "dudes."

"Give me a shout next time you need some help," the
blond guy says, walking away. Sebastian turns toward us
with a look of apology on his face. Just before the guy steps
off the curb, he turns back toward us. "Later, dudes!" he
yells.

Sebastian shakes his head. "Jacob knows at least eleven
common ways to use the word *dude* in a sentence."

"A few uncommon ways too," Sarah says. "You should
have seen Mr. Simmons's face every time Jacob called
him dude."

Fig starts laughing. "Mr. Simmons is the man in the
suit," she says to me. "Sebastian's dad."

"You mean the *dude* in the suit," Sarah says.

"So," Sebastian says, bending over the duffle bag. "You
dudes want to get something to eat?"

"Didn't you just eat?" Fig asks.

"I'm hungry," I say, surprising myself. Sebastian grins
and offers me a fist bump. I find myself smiling back.

Fig shrugs. "Lunch it is," she says. "So, what's in the
bag?" she asks, gesturing to the duffle.

Sebastian frowns. "What *was* in the bag is the question."

He pulls it open and steps aside so we can see. Inside are dozens of boxes of sugar cubes. Most of them are crushed.

A policeman cycles over and stops in front of us. "You guys need to clear out." He gestures at the sign, which I can read now that I'm closer. The permit's only until four o'clock.

"Sure thing, dude," Sebastian says, earning him a frown. "I mean, sir."

"What's your next stunt?" the policeman asks.

"I'm going to build a bed out of sugar cubes and sleep on it in the middle of Times Square," he says.

"That I have to see," the policeman says. He waits while we gather all of Sebastian's stuff, including an extra container of soup, a cantaloupe, and a Super Soaker water gun.

"What's this for?" I ask.

"Don't ask," Sarah says, seeing my face. "It involves pudding." She shakes her head. "Totally nasty." Sebastian returns the sandwich board to the store on the corner where he must have borrowed it. He returns, smiling.

"Guy gave me twenty bucks," he says. "Said it was the best advertising he's ever had."

"Maybe they'll sponsor you," Fig says. "You could go pro."

"I want to keep my amateur status," Sebastian says.

"Why? In case they make eating an Olympic sport?" Fig asks. "Speaking of food . . ."

"Let's get pizza," Sarah says. She digs in her pocket. "I have money," she says, pulling out a ten-dollar bill. I reach into my back pocket for what I have left of the money my dad gave me.

"Seventeen," I say.

"That's more than enough," Fig says. She looks at Sebastian. "Okay, maybe just enough."

We start walking, Fig and Sebastian in front and Sarah and me in back. Sarah starts asking me questions, one right after the other. What kind of music do I listen to? What was it like living in Maine? What's my family like? How did it feel to meet my grandmother for the first time?

"Weird," I say, answering the last question.

Sarah sighs. "Our grandmother's pretty weird too," Sarah says. "She thinks she's Marilyn Monroe." I glance over at her, not sure if she's joking. She smirks at me. "Well, at least she does when she's off her meds."

I'm not sure how to react, but Sarah keeps talking, telling me about all kinds of things, like how last fall Sebastian carved seventeen jack o' lanterns in four minutes and how Fig got a bunch of artists to do ice sculptures in Central Park at Christmas. "Fig can convince anyone to do just about anything," Sarah says.

"But I always use my power for good and not evil," Fig says from in front of us. I remember Sebastian's comment about her bat ears.

"Just wait," Sarah says. "She'll have you doing something soon enough."

I think of having to dress as a giant cannoli in only four days and nod.

"Where's Cooper?" I ask. I try to make my voice casual, and I guess it works because Sarah just shrugs. "Around," she says. "Working maybe or—" She stops talking.

At first, I think it's because we're in front of the pizza place, but then I see her frown a little as if considering whether to tell me something more. "He's probably working," she says, clearly deciding not to share more information.

I hold the door while everyone walks inside, then follow them in. As we walk to the table, everyone starts giving their pizza topping choices. "Pineapple," I say. I half listen to what everyone else wants as we sit down, because the other half of me is thinking about Sarah's face, wondering if everyone has something to hide. I think about Fig and her secrets and her inability to actually keep any. And then about my sister and her secrets, and me and mine. And I wonder what would happen if we simply decided not to keep everything secret any longer. Just like that.

The streetlights are all on by the time I get back to my grandmother's. I slide the key into the lock, but the door is pulled out of my hand before I have a chance to open it.

"Where have you been?" my grandmother demands. Her arms are folded, but her eyes seem more worried than angry.

"I left you a note," I say, sidestepping the question. She raises an eyebrow at me as if to say that she knows I'm sidestepping, but she's letting it go *this time.* I follow her inside.

"I thought we'd have dinner together," she says.

"Oh," I say, surprised. It's my turn to raise my eyebrow, but she's already turned away from me and is walking toward the kitchen. This is the first time she's shown much interest in spending any time with me at all. She directs me to set the table, which I do, but I obviously do it wrong, because when she comes in, she moves the glass from above the fork to above where the spoon and knife are resting.

"Your mother used to always get that wrong too," she says. She speaks softly, almost as if she's talking to herself instead of to me.

She holds her hands in front of her and makes the *okay* sign with both of them. "The drink goes on the right." She lifts her hand slightly. "See how my right hand makes a letter d?"

I nod.

"D for drink," she says.

"And your left hand?" I ask.

"B for bread," she says, making me feel like I'm in the middle of a Sesame Street episode. "You put the bread plate here."

"What about B for beverage?" I ask.

She shakes her head. "Also like your mother." She heads back into the kitchen, leaving me to marvel at this tiny discovery. My mother's life before she met my father was always off-limits. Other than a couple of tattered novels filled with margin notes, I have no idea what she was like when she was younger.

We eat dinner, which is actually really good. Vegetable soup and salad with pears and pecans. I try to follow her lead as we eat, but she keeps frowning over at me. All the scrutiny and all the frowning are making me so nervous that I'm barely able to get the soup to my mouth without dribbling all over the place. I should tell Sebastian that his new trick should be eating soup with my grandmother. I'd like to see him do *that* without spilling any.

Veronica instructs me to hold my fork in my left hand and slice the pear with my knife in my right. "Don't keep switching hands," she says, demonstrating. She lifts her fork to her mouth with her left hand. "Switching is so *American*. So *provincial*." I want to say that we actually are in America and that where I grew up in Maine is about as provincial as it gets, but I keep my mouth shut.

During the course of the meal, Veronica instructs me on how to butter my bread (not in my hand and not directly from the butter dish). I'll have to remember to tell my father that he's been eating his toast all wrong for years. Thinking about him makes my stomach hurt.

I try to think of something to distract myself. "What is this fork for?" I ask, pointing to the one lying sideways above my plate.

"Dessert," she says.

"What's for dessert?" I ask.

"Pie," she says. Well, that sounds promising. I love

pie. Love probably isn't a strong enough word for my feelings about pie. Rachel used to make up sayings about it. *Preoccupied with pie. Passionate for pie. Possessed by pie. Proclivity for pie.* I even have a shirt with I ? on the front of it.

"If you'll help clear, I'll get dessert," Veronica says. I manage to clear the table without breaking anything. She brings the pie to the table along with two plates and a silver pie server. The pie looks a little strange.

"Did you make this?" I ask.

"A friend did," Veronica says, passing me a piece. I wait until she has a slice in front of her and has taken a bite. You always wait. At least I know that much. I take a bite, and then look at my pie. It not only looks strange, it tastes strange. I look up at Veronica, who is also staring at her plate.

"What kind of pie is this again?" I ask.

"Raw chocolate pie," Veronica says. She looks at me. "It's made with avocados."

And I can't be sure, but I think I hear laughter in her voice somewhere. I try to fix a polite look on my face, but apparently, I don't succeed.

"It's awful," my grandmother says.

I nod. It is completely awful. Then she smiles over at me and I'm grinning back. And it's like a miracle.

But then, *blink*, it's gone, like a light being switched off. We both look at the slightly greenish pie on the table between us. Veronica gets up and takes the remainder of the pie into the kitchen. I hear the water and then the sound of the garbage disposal. I stare at the remains of the pie on my plate. I wish Rachel were here for this momentous occasion. She would pretend to be shocked that I found a pie I didn't like. Then we'd take turns figuring out new names for the pie. *Peculiar pie. Puce pie. Putrid pie. Possibly poisonous pie.*

I'm smiling just thinking about her, and then I remember that because of what I did, Rachel won't ever smile again. I have to close my eyes and remind myself that I'm not allowed to cry.

Pitiful. Pestilent. Pathetic. Poison.

Chapter Seven

For my birthday last year, we had lemon meringue pie. I also received three gifts. The first was a camera, a nice one. When I first announced I wanted to learn photography, they said I had to start on my dad's old Nikon because I had to understand photography before I could take good photos. The camera they gave me for my birthday was my first digital one. I dropped the batteries in, slid in the memory card, and turned it on. I aimed it across the table at Rachel with the usual "smile," but what I got was a scrunched-up nose and a tongue sticking out at me.

Rachel gave me an empty locket. "You have to figure out what to put in it," she said, winking at me.

The third present was a box of cards from my mother. Each one had a question on it. I pulled one out at random.

"If you could change one thing in your life, what would it be?" I asked.

"I'd like to have more hair," my father said, running his hand over the rapidly expanding bald spot at the back of his head. My mother kissed him on the spot after he said it, making him smile and me and Rachel groan.

"Ew," Rachel said. "Keep it PG. There are minors present."

"I wouldn't change anything," my mother said, looking at all of us. "Not one thing."

I turned to Rachel. "World peace?" she replied.

"Lame," I said. "It has to be something personal. Something just about you."

"Does it say that on the card?" she asked, trying to pull it away from me. I held it away from her so she couldn't get it. "Okay," she said. "I wish I were more like you."

"Fine," I said. "If you aren't going to take this seriously, you can't play." Popular, beautiful Rachel, who everyone loved, wanted to be like me. Not likely.

"Okay, smarty, what about you?" Rachel asked. She took a bite of my birthday pie and looked at me.

I could think of about seventeen things I'd like to have different in my life. I think I said something lame like I wanted better hair or I wanted to be taller. If someone asked me that question now, I'd only have one answer. I'd change the rest of that whole night. From the moment we headed out into the darkness to go to her friend's house right through to the next morning.

"We're aren't going to Stacy's," Rachel had said, putting the car in gear and pulling out of the driveway.

"Okay," I said. "Then where are we going?"

"Think of it as a second birthday party," Rachel said, "But with less pie and more fun."

I remember digging my fingernails into my palms, excited that Rachel was taking me with her somewhere and scared that I wouldn't be cool enough for her friends. I was also afraid of getting in trouble with our parents.

"Relax," Rachel said, grabbing my hand and giving it a squeeze. She smiled at me and I knew it was going to be okay. I trusted her implicitly.

If I concentrate hard enough, I can still almost feel the pressure of her hand in mine, her warm fingers on my cold hand.

Cannoli Day arrives much too quickly.

"I can't breathe," I say, pulling the fabric away from my face.

"Hush," Fig says, leading me through the crowded diner and out onto the sidewalk. She has to lead me because with the cannoli mask on, I have no peripheral vision. I pull at the fabric again, feeling hot and breathless and claustrophobic.

"Stop," Fig says, adjusting the headpiece that is supposed to be the cream filling spilling out of the end of the dessert. "It looks weird when you do that."

I snort in a non-cannoli-like fashion. "Yes, because I don't already look weird enough dressed up as a giant Italian pastry."

This makes Fig laugh, which makes me laugh, and soon I'm bent over with my hands resting on my fabric-covered knees and my cream filling threatening to drop off my head and onto the sidewalk.

"Girls!" someone hisses behind me. I have to turn all the way around to see Grace, standing with her hands on her hips. "Keep it together."

I nod, making my filling wobble. Fig giggles again behind me. It's a good thing I can't see her. I'm afraid if I could, I'd never stop laughing. But the thought of all my oxygen disappearing in an uncontrollable laughing fit is enough to sober me.

I spend the next few hours waving at passing cars, shaking hands with little kids—who either run crying from the giant dessert or who want their picture taken with me—and trying to stay out of the way. Once my discomfort fades, I realize this may not be the worst job in the world. Dressed in the costume, I feel more normal than I have in more than a year. I can laugh and talk to people without them seeing me, and being hidden is oddly freeing. Sure, everyone is still staring at me, but this time it's because I'm dressed like a crazy pastry, not because of my scar.

My phone buzzes in my back pocket, and I wonder if it's another photo from my dad. Besides Fig, he's the only person who texts me—my mom has maintained radio silence since our awkward phone call. In addition to the sand dollar, over the past couple of days Dad's sent me a photo of a sunset partially obscured by one of his flip-flopped feet and another of a chocolate-sprinkle donut bisected by his thumb. I try to distance myself from his texts, but I feel something shift in my heart each time my phone buzzes.

I tell myself that I'll check my phone as soon as I can. I'm pretty sure Grace would freak if the giant cannoli starting texting.

Part of what makes Cannoli Day so popular is that Brunelli's sells them for ten cents each, which is what they cost eighty years ago when Brunelli's first opened. People keep buying them by the boxful. After one guy leaves with six dozen, Nonna puts a limit on how many people can buy. Even with the limit, it's all Joey can do to keep the shells coming out of the kitchen so Grace and Gina and Nonna can fill them and box them up.

Just before lunch, Cooper shows up. He and Sebastian stand off to one side, leaning against the side of the building. Fig nods in their direction. Because of the stupid headpiece, I have to turn all the way around to see them. Sebastian walks up to Nonna, who smiles and tries to ruffle his hair, but I think dreadlocks are impossible to ruffle by definition. She gives him a cannoli. Fig hands him another cannoli, and he munches on it while he talks to her.

"So, where's Mia?" he asks.

Fig pretends to look around. "I don't know," she says.

"She was right here a minute ago." I smile underneath the costume. I really am anonymous in this thing.

Cooper walks over to stand next to Sebastian. He grabs the other cannoli out of Sebastian's hand and bites it, then looks straight at me. "Hey, Mia," he says.

Sebastian turns quickly and scrutinizes me, then he frowns at Fig, who starts laughing.

"Hi," I say, my voice pushed back at me by the costume.

"How did you know it was her?" Fig asks. Cooper shrugs and takes another bite of his cannoli. He glances at me briefly, and I feel my cheeks get hot.

"Move it or lose it," Grace says, putting another tray of cannoli shells on the table in front of us.

"Guess we should—" Sebastian begins.

Fig leans toward him. "Go inside and tell Joey that you heard his minestrone wasn't as good as the soup at Lombardi's." She says it softly.

"What? So, I can get my head bashed in?" Sebastian asks. "Have you seen the size of that guy?"

"Trust me," Fig says. He looks at her, concerned, but then nods and hits Cooper lightly on the arm, gesturing toward the front door. I watch them walk into the diner. A little boy starts yelling that he wants to touch the giant dessert.

Nonna decides it's time to move Cannoli Day inside. It's getting hotter by the second. And even if I'm not that savvy about the whole cannoli thing, I do know that hot days and pastry cream don't mix. Fig and I walk through the diner, where Sebastian and Cooper are sitting at the counter with big, steaming bowls of soup in front of them and Joey towering over both. Fig just smiles and waves as we pass. Grace told me not to take off the costume until we were in the kitchen. Like we don't want to spoil the illusion that the giant cannoli might be real. Fig helps me pull off the headpiece and unzips the back of the costume so I can pull it off.

Without the costume, I immediately feel exposed again. I pull it off myself, dropping my chin and trying not to look at Fig as I put the costume back on its hanger.

"It's hot," Fig says. I nod. I'm so sweaty that my hair is sticking to the back of my neck. "Come on," she says, leading me through the kitchen and into the walk-in cooler. We stand there until our teeth are chattering and we have to rub our arms to keep warm.

"So, how was it?" Fig asks.

I shrug, smiling slightly. "I wouldn't want to wear it every day, but it wasn't that bad."

Fig rolls her eyes. "No, I mean seeing Cooper again."

"Stop," I say. I feign a sudden interest in the wheels of cheese stacked on one of the shelves. "How do they get all that wax on them?" I ask.

Fig stares at me long enough to let me know she's giving me an out, but that I'm not totally off the hook. I half wonder if she got my grandmother to teach her that look. "Well, I'm no cheeseologist," Fig says, "but I assume dipping."

I nod like what she said just solved one of life's mysteries for me.

"Tomorrow night, Sarah's playing at The Wall," Fig says. "You want to go?" She narrows her eyes at me. "Unless, of course, you have other plans."

"What's The Wall?" I ask.

Fig shrugs. "A hipster coffee house where they have open mic. It's a mixed bag, but Sarah's really good."

"I'll have to check my calendar," I say, playing along. Part of me wishes I did have plans. The thought of going out at night to a coffee house where there will be a lot of people freaks me out. At least maybe it'll be dark in there.

I'm really shivering now. I reach for the door, but Fig puts her hand on my arm.

"Listen," she says. "Cooper's a great guy, but he's sort of . . ." She looks around at the cheese and condiments stacked on the shelves surrounding us as if trying to find a good adjective to describe him. I raise my eyebrows. She sees the look on my face and smiles slightly. "All I mean is that he can be hard to get to know."

"He seems nice," I say.

She nods. "He's great, but he disappears a lot." She shrugs. "Sarah says he just needs space sometimes."

"Did you ever? I mean, did you guys ever—"

"If you're asking if I dated Cooper, then the answer is no. When I met Cooper, he was . . . Well, he was unavailable." She pushes the door open and we walk back into the kitchen. I use my fingers to comb my hair down so that it covers the side of my face. "Besides, that's when I met Sebastian. There's just something about a guy who can put away as much food as he can." She grins goofily at me, and I can't help but smile back.

Fig heads into Nonna's office and I pull out my phone. I open up the text and click the photo. It's of a sign. *Fish Sandwiches & Live Bait Sold Here.* My dad's thumb is across the lens of his phone. I reply with a heart emoji. It's a deal I made with myself—I am allowed to reply, but not actually initiate contact. I slide my phone back into my pocket just as Fig comes out of the office. She motions for me to follow her to the front. Sebastian and Cooper are still sitting at the counter, now with sandwiches in front of them.

"Can you believe this guy had the nerve to say my minestrone wasn't as good as Lombardi's?" Joey says, hitching his thumb in Sebastian's direction. Fig pretends to look shocked. Joey turns to Cooper and Sebastian. "Now who has the better soup?"

"You do," Sebastian says, around a bite of sandwich.

"Definitely," Cooper says, nodding. Joey just dips his head as if that settles it, then walks down to the end of the counter and starts rearranging the tubs of peppers and onions.

"See?" Fig says, smiling at them. Both Cooper and Sebastian grin.

"I'm glad you came out when you did," Cooper says. "I was afraid he wouldn't stop feeding us." He looks down at his plate and the remaining half a sandwich.

"You gonna eat that?" Sebastian asks. He takes it before Cooper has a chance to answer. "You ready to head over to Eddie's?" he asks Fig. She nods and reaches under the counter for her bag. Sebastian stands, still clutching the sandwich. He takes a giant bite. Then another.

"Eddie's is an art supply store over on Houston," Fig tells me. Sebastian pushes the last of his sandwich into his mouth.

"You guys wanna come?" he asks when he finishes swallowing. He looks from me to Cooper as he wipes his mouth with a napkin before crumpling it and putting it on the now empty plate.

"I've got to work," Cooper says. He glances over at me and then away, and I think about what Fig said about him needing space. Then he turns to me. "Want to come with me?" he asks. "I have to . . ."

I'm bobbing my head before he finishes, making him smile. I walk back into the kitchen and grab my bag. When I come back out, Sebastian and Fig are gone, but Cooper's standing near the front. He holds the door for me. I duck my chin a little as I pass, careful to let my hair fall across my cheek. I walk on the right side of him as we head farther downtown.

I look at him out of the corner of my eye. Cooper seems so easy with his mouth. I never see him try to hide it or cover it or anything. Maybe when you've had something all your life, you get used to it.

"Do you like dogs?" Cooper asks. He looks over at me and I nod. "Good thing," he says. "Good thing."

Chapter Eight

When Cooper asked if I liked dogs, I was thinking theoretical dogs, not actual dogs and definitely not seven of them.

"Here," he says. "Take this." He hands me a leash with hooks all along both sides of it. We go from building to building picking up dogs. He takes them after we pick up three—I gratefully hand them off. Clearly you need more experience than I have navigating the narrow sidewalks with dogs going off in every direction. I have to hold them each time Cooper goes to retrieve a new one. Mostly we get buzzed in by *the staff*, as Cooper calls them, but he has keys to two of the places.

"I haven't even met the owners of most of these dogs," he says as we walk. "Just the maid or the nanny."

He clips the dogs to the leash I'm holding as we pick them up. There's a Saint Bernard and a lab and a terrier thing that barks constantly. There's a tiny Chihuahua that gets her own leash (pink with rhinestones) and a basset hound with ears so long, they drag on the ground. We pick up a greyhound, who Cooper tells me is really nice, but a couple of sandwiches short of a picnic. After being clipped in alongside the others, he just stares at me with his sweet, vacant eyes.

The last dog we pick up is in a basement apartment of a run-down building. An older woman comes to the door and hands Cooper the leash. At the end of it is a beautiful Irish setter. The dog is so happy to see Cooper that he just runs around him in a circle, wrapping the leash around and around his knees. Cooper laughs and untwists himself. He leads the dog back up to the sidewalk to where I'm waiting, attempting to keep six dogs under control.

"This is Waffles," he says. Waffles makes a chuffing noise at the sound of his name.

"Waffles?" I ask, smiling. Cooper shrugs. "Hi, Waffles," I say, bending down and letting him sniff my hand.

"He's mine. I mean, Sarah's and mine."

"Is that where you live?" I ask, pointing down the steps to where the door is just now closing.

Cooper rubs the back of his neck and looks past me. "Sort of," he says.

I wait for more, but he just bends down and attaches Waffles's collar to the chain of dogs that I'm already holding. Then he rolls up Waffles's leash and slips it into his pocket.

The loaded leash feels like what I imagine holding a dogsled team would be like. Then he trades me. He lets me walk the Chihuahua while he takes the rest of the pack.

"You okay?" he asks, nodding at the dog I'm holding.

"I got this," I say.

"Just be careful of other dogs and people and cars and everything else."

"I got this," I repeat. I mean, how difficult could one dog be?

"Seriously," he says. "Just be careful." I tilt my head at Cooper. "Trust me," he says.

And though it seems stupid, because I don't really even know him that well, something in his voice and his eyes makes me trust him. Or at least want to.

"Where to?" I ask, letting the Chihuahua pull me down the sidewalk.

"I usually take them over to the park," he says.

He walks beside me, so close I can feel the heat of his arm on mine. A woman is walking toward us, alternating between talking on her phone and sipping from her cup of coffee. Cooper falls back so that I can move over and let her pass.

"Stop it," he says from behind me.

I glance back and see the bassett hound trying to scoop up a fallen hot dog bun. I draw even with the lady, and the Chihuahua goes bananas. She tries to lunge at the woman, and bite through her leash, her collar, and my shoe all at the same time. It isn't until the woman is nearly all the way to the corner that the dog stops freaking out.

"See?" Cooper says, grimacing at me.

We turn at the corner and enter the park. Several people sit, hunched over chess games at the tables. Cooper points to the other end of the park, where there is a fence and a big sign with more than a dozen rules for dog owners. The Chihuahua pulls me toward the entrance. The other dogs and Cooper are close behind. They all wait, mostly patiently, for me to unclip them. As I do, each of them runs into the park. Once the leash is empty, I roll it around my hand and stand up. Cooper unhooks the Chihuahua, who immediately goes at the Saint Bernard, who's holding a stick.

"Samson is such a bully," Cooper says. I watch the Saint Bernard, but he is just standing there while the Chihuahua turns into a barking, yapping whirlwind around him.

"He seems pretty mellow," I say.

Cooper smiles at me. "Samson is the Chihuahua."

"Samson. It's a warrior's name," I say.

"He's had four names in as many months," Cooper says. "He's a mess."

The Chihuahua moves from dog to dog, attacking them or stealing their toys. More than once Cooper has to go over and grab Samson and put him in a timeout. Timeout for Samson means Cooper holds him up at arm's length until he stops freaking out. When he's released, he behaves for about five seconds before he starts attacking the next dog.

"You have to give him props for bravery," I say, watching him square off against a Doberman over a tennis ball.

"Stupidity often seems like bravery," Cooper says.

I look over at him. Something in his voice suggests we might not be talking about Samson anymore. We watch the dogs play for a while in silence, but it's not an uncomfortable one. It's just sort of quiet. Well, quiet except for the dozens of dogs running in every direction and barking their heads off. After about twenty minutes, Waffles comes over and sits on Cooper's foot. Cooper bends and puts his hand on the dog's head.

"You tired, buddy?" he asks, scratching behind his ears.

Cooper looks back toward the park and sighs. I follow his gaze. Samson has the basset hound cornered. He's lunging and snapping at his ears. Cooper moves Waffles off his foot, and Waffles promptly shifts to sit on mine. Cooper goes over and picks up Samson, who turns on him in an instant, trying to bite his hands and face. He holds Samson against his chest with one hand while he checks to make sure the basset hound is all right. When the dog nuzzles Cooper's hand, Cooper smiles and ruffles his long ears. The basset hound trundles off to play a moment later, finding some doggy friends who aren't quite so aggressive. Cooper returns to me, still clutching Samson. He puts him on his leash and holds him close.

"I hate bullies," he says. He turns and closes his eyes for a second and takes a deep breath. When he opens his eyes, he smiles down at Waffles, still sitting on my foot. "He likes you," he says.

"How can you tell?" I ask.

"It's the foot-sitting. He only does that when he really likes someone." Cooper shrugs. "It's odd, but it's his thing."

Part of me wonders what Cooper's "thing" is.

"It's sort of a weird job," I say, trying to change the subject. "Dog walking, I mean."

Cooper looks at me, still holding tight to Samson's collar. "How so?"

"It's just sort of weird how people get these animals, knowing they can't take care of them, but it's okay because there's this whole system that will take care of their pet for them."

"So, I'm part of the system?" Cooper asks me.

"Everyone is," I say. "You. The dogs. The owners. It's like this big system designed to let people have what they want without any responsibility."

"Maybe they realize they aren't the best ones to take care of their dogs," Cooper says.

"Then why get them?" I ask. "Why have something if you're not going to take care of it?"

Cooper shrugs. "Probably some of them mean well, but at some point, they realize they just can't."

"Can't?" I ask. "Or won't?"

Cooper sighs. "Both, probably."

"So when they're just too much of a hassle or it gets inconvenient, or maybe the dog makes a mistake, they just dump her on someone else?"

Too late, I realize I just said *her*. Cooper looks at me for a long moment, and I feel like I did when he knew it was me wearing the costume. That he knows me just by looking at me.

"Sorry," I say. "I didn't mean to go off."

"I like people who aren't afraid to say what they're thinking," Cooper says. He smiles at me for a moment before turning his attention back to the dogs. Cooper gives a whistle, which the dogs must recognize, because all of them except the basset hound come over.

"Will you go get him?" Cooper asks, taking the multi-leash from me. "He's a little deaf."

I walk over to the basset hound, who has his back turned to me. I put my hand out and touch him softly on the back so I don't startle him, but he jumps anyway. He turns and stares at me with his mournful eyes, and then he gets up and follows me, trusting I'll take him where he needs to go. I walk back to where Cooper is trying to hold Samson with one hand while clipping all the other dogs to the leash. I help him by holding on to Samson, who must have tired himself out, because he's acting mostly normal.

Waffles sits on my foot again while we wait for Cooper to finish clicking all the dogs in. I look down at Waffles and think about how he likes me without even knowing me. And I wonder if he did know me, would he still like me? Maybe, I think. Dogs just do that. But people?

I glance at Cooper out of the corner of my eye, but he's staring at the mass of dogs swirling in front of us. I wonder if he really knew me, knew what was inside, would *he* still like me? With dogs, you pretty much get what you see. I used to think people were the same way, but now I think most people are really two people—the person on the inside that we keep hidden, and the person on the outside that we dress up and fix up and show to the world as a form of protection.

Sometimes I feel like the person on the inside of me is just going to fade away and all I'll be left with is a hollow shell.

Chapter Nine

There's a note on the kitchen counter when I get back to my grandmother's apartment.

Your father called.

I check my cell, thinking I might not have heard it ring with all the barking, but there are no missed calls. Photos, yes. Words, no.

I sit down in Veronica's reading chair by the window. From where I'm sitting, there's a pretty good view of the building next to us. I stand up and press my forehead against the glass; all I can see is the edge of the alley that separates Veronica's building from the one next to it. I unlatch the window and try to raise it. I'm not really expecting it to move as I pull it, but it does, and I lean out in an attempt to see anything else. With my head out, I can view more of the alleyway—a dumpster and trash, and a chair with only three legs. To the left, there's just more alleyway and a thin strip of light where it ends in the next street, but when I turn to the right, I smile. If I lean a little farther out, I can see the Brooklyn Bridge and a tiny slice of water. For some reason, seeing that makes me happy, like there's something bigger beyond this apartment and this building and this block. Something bigger beyond me.

There's a noise behind me. I pull my head in and look.

"What are you doing?" Veronica is standing in the doorway, her keys clutched in one hand and her purse in the other. She looks very pale.

"Did you know you can see the bridge from here?" I ask. I poke my head back out and look right again. Soon there are footsteps behind me. I pull my head back in and look at my grandmother, who looks even worse up close. "What's wrong?" I ask.

"You were just looking at the view?" Veronica asks. Her voice trembles a little.

"What did you think I was doing?" I ask.

Her eyes flood with tears. I open my mouth to say something more, but she's already turning away from me, brushing at her cheeks. I look down at the alleyway far below me and then I walk into the kitchen, where Veronica is filling up the kettle at the sink.

"I was just looking at the view," I confirm.

"Of course you were," Veronica says, putting the kettle on the stove. Her voice is calm, but her hand is shaking slightly, making the water in the kettle slosh against its sides.

"I'm not a threat to myself or others," I say, attempting to joke with her.

"Of course you aren't." She looks at me, uncertainty in her eyes. It makes me wonder what my father told her. But then her mask slips back into place. Whatever she was thinking or feeling is buried again.

"Do you want some tea?" she asks, taking two cups from the cabinet without waiting for an answer.

"Yes," I say. "Please."

She looks at me for a long moment, and I can see the mask slip just a tiny bit again, but she gives herself a little shake, like she's reminding herself to keep it together. The gesture seems familiar, and I realize it's the same move my mother developed last year. Like she was a snow globe that needed to keep the snow swirling enough to hide what was inside.

"I'm going to go freshen up," Veronica says. "Will you keep an eye on the kettle?"

I say I will and watch her walk out of the kitchen and down the hall toward her room. She pulls the door shut behind her. When the kettle whistles, I pour the steaming water into the teapot she has waiting on the counter. I wait for a few minutes, but when Veronica doesn't come back, I walk over to her closed door. I lift my hand to knock, to tell her that the tea's ready, but a noise from within stops me. I lean in a little and listen, then I pull back and quietly walk back to the kitchen.

When I crawl into bed hours later, exhausted from the day, I can still hear the sounds echoing in my head.

The sound of crying behind a closed door.

Even though I want to hear Sarah play and even though I know Cooper will be there, I try to get out of going to The Wall. Fig tells me it will be dark. *No, not pitch black.* And that hardly anyone will be there. *Manhattan hardly anyone. Not Downeast Maine hardly anyone.* I tell Fig my grandmother might need me, but Fig has Nonna call Veronica and get her okay, which, truthfully, I probably had all along. Finally, Fig corners me in the cooler when I go in to get Joey more jam.

"What's really going on, Mia?" she asks. She stands in the open doorway with her arms folded. I look at the jar of strawberry jam I'm holding, thinking.

"Close the door!" Grace shouts at us as she walks through. I start to go past Fig and out into the kitchen, but Fig just pulls the door closed behind her, shutting us both in.

"Tell me," she says. I keep turning the jar in my hands, watching the pieces of strawberry shift inside. "If you don't want to hang out with us, just say it."

That makes me look up. She's staring at the stacks of cheese just behind me. "Fig," I say. "Look at me." She moves her gaze to my face.

"Okay," she says when I don't say anything.

"No," I say. "Really look at my face." I turn my head to the left, so the whole right side of my face is toward her.

"Mia, I know," she says quietly.

"Do you?" I ask. "Do you really know what it's like to have people stare at you?"

"Yeah," she says softly. "I do." Something about the way she says it makes me pause. We stand there looking at each other for a few moments before Grace yanks the door open.

"Break's over, ladies," she says. She holds the door open for us as we walk back into the kitchen.

I head toward the door, to where Joey is waiting for the jam. Fig puts a hand on my arm. I look over at her. "Just come," she says.

Fig was right about one thing: the coffee house is dark. But she was hugely wrong about one thing. There aren't "like seven" people there as she said. More like seven hundred. I say this to her. She gives me a look.

"Okay, more like two hundred," I say.

"Mia, there are probably like forty people here. Tops." She hands me a mug of coffee, nodding toward the counter that contains pitchers of milk and packets of sugar and eco-friendly napkins. I walk over and I stand there, looking at all the options. I've never been much of a coffee drinker.

Fig joins me and shakes some sugar into her mug and adds a stream of milk. I take a sip from my mug and make a face. "Here." She hands me the milk. I add enough to make the black coffee turn tan. "And here," she says, handing me a packet of raw sugar. I pour it in and stir.

I take another sip. Better, but still pretty nasty. "It's so bitter," I say.

"You get used to it," she says.

"Doesn't that seem sort of twisted?" I ask. "You drink something foul until you get used to the taste?"

"Ah, the irony of being a grown-up," Fig says. "You do things that you don't like until you do like them, and then you complain that you can't stop."

We walk toward an empty table off to one side. "It's the same with beer," I say, thinking of the one beer I've ever had.

"Beer?" she asks. She looks at me funny. Instantly, I regret mentioning it.

"One," I say.

She nods. "You didn't seem like the type."

"The beer-drinking type?" I ask.

She shrugs and takes a sip from her mug. "A partier," she says.

"I'm definitely not a partier," I respond, thinking of the one and only *party* I've ever been to.

A guy in tight black jeans and black Chucks steps onto the stage. He starts rearranging stools and microphones and random boxes full of extra mugs and bags of coffee and reams of napkins.

Fig waves at Sebastian, who has just walked in. He smiles over at us. "Be right back," she says.

She joins him at the counter, and he puts his hand on the middle of her back while they stand there. Seeing that makes my heart ache. Hardly anyone's really touched me in almost a year, other than a couple of perfunctory hugs and pats from my parents. I'm untouchable.

Sebastian and Fig walk over. He sets his mug on the table and grins at me. "I'm glad you decided to come." The way he says it makes me know he and Fig talked about how I was trying to get out of coming tonight.

"I wouldn't miss it," I say, looking over at Fig. She takes a sip of her coffee, but her eyes are smiling at me.

Sebastian sits next to Fig and puts his arm around her chair. He's not actually touching her, but I still feel the same bump in my heart.

"Have you seen Sarah yet?" Sebastian asks.

Fig shakes her head. "You know how she is."

Sebastian looks at me. "She has stage fright. Bad." I tilt my head at this. "I mean puking, hyperventilating bad."

"Then why does she do it?" I ask.

Sebastian looks at me for a long moment. "Did you bring your camera tonight?"

"I did," I say.

"Why?" he asks.

"Because—" I begin, not sure how to answer.

He smiles at me. "Exactly. Because you have to. Because your photography is a part of you." I nod slowly. "Even if it was hard for you to take photos, you still would." I nod again, thinking, *if only he knew how hard.* "It's like a fire shut up in your bones."

Fig shakes her head. "He's just quoting Cooper," she says.

"It's not like Cooper made that up," Sebastian complains.

The guy on the stage taps the microphone, silencing everyone. "Welcome to Open Mic Night," he says. A few people clap. "First up, Tyler White." A burst of applause from a table on the other side of the room makes me jump.

Fig rolls her eyes. "Tyler White is such a poser."

"Hipster doofus," Sebastian says.

Tyler White steps onto the stage and stands silently in front of the microphone. Then he begins chanting. It's not English.

"Romulan," Sebastian says. I shake my head, confused. "As in *Star Trek.*"

Fig shakes her head. "Poser." I nod. We have to endure nearly ten minutes of Tyler. After the chanting comes poetry. Original. Bad.

"Okay," the emcee guy says, taking the stage again. "Let's hear it for Tyler White."

The table near the back erupts with whistles and clapping. I turn and see a whole table filled with Tyler clones, both male and female.

The emcee guy clears his throat and the table settles down. "Next up is Sarah Callum."

He steps away from the mic as Sarah walks forward from the other side of the stage with a guitar clutched in one hand. She looks very pale and very small. I pull my camera out. switch it on, and make sure the flash is off. Sarah stands in front of the microphone and closes her eyes. I look over at the opposite wall and see Cooper standing there. His eyes meet mine, and then he looks back at Sarah, who is still standing silently in front of the microphone with her eyes still closed. I zoom in and click once, twice, then turn my camera off. She shifts her guitar and strums a chord, and then she leans toward the microphone.

Her singing is breathless and soft. The lyrics are of home and love. Then they turn dark, and her words are of loss and pain. But at the end, she repeats the same phrase a bit softer each time until it's little more than a whisper.

Then we were beautiful.

Then we were beautiful.

Sarah steps away from the microphone. The only sound is the hiss of the milk steamer and the steady rumble of cars driving past. Sarah walks to the edge of the stage. Fig is the first on her feet, clapping. Sebastian and I both follow. Then one by one, people all around us are standing and clapping. Even the barista has stopped making coffee and is clapping. I'm surprised to see tears on Fig's cheeks. And more surprised to feel them on my own.

Chapter Ten

My dad left first. He signed up for advanced ballistics training last fall, training that my mother said he didn't even need. I was back in the hospital at that point for another surgery. He came in to tell me he was going. Talked to me while he looked at the floor, out the window, at the machine dripping saline into my arm. He never looked at me, even when he said he'd miss me and patted my leg through the thin blanket. He called a lot during that trip, almost every night. I was only in the hospital for two days that time, so I was home for most of them. Sometimes he and my mother would be on the phone a long time, but sometimes she'd just hand the phone to me. It was hard with him gone. The house was too big. The rooms too empty.

But it was worse when he got back. We're not yellers in my family; we're stuffers. We just push down whatever is bothering us. The problem is when you're too full and you keep pushing. It's like a garbage bag bursting. All the trash spews out and goes all over everything.

I remember the day the bag burst.

They stood in the hallway—my father at one end, my mother at the other. Framed photos of our family hung on the walls between them. They thought I was out walking, but I sat on my bed, the teddy bear I've had since I was two years old clutched in my arms.

"I just can't do it anymore!" my mother said, her voice hard and low.

"What?" my father asked. "Be married? Be a mother?" I held my breath and closed my eyes.

"Yes," my mother said softly.

"Yes, to which?" my father asked.

"Both," my mother said. I felt the heat behind them. "I'm sorry, David," she said, her voice barely a whisper. The whispering was worse.

"Is that what you're going to tell Mia?" my father asked. "That you're *sorry*?"

My mother didn't respond. I breathed deeply, smelling the antiseptic they'd sprayed on my bear so I could keep him with me in the hospital.

"What am I supposed to do?" my mother finally asked.

"You're supposed to keep going," my father said. "Just like the rest of us."

"David," my mother said, slowly. "I can't. It just hurts too much."

"You're not the only one hurting, Kate."

A loon called from the lake behind our house. A warning trill. The machine gun call of danger. I touched the long scar along my cheek, drawing my finger down the length of it.

"I know," my mother said quietly. "I know you're hurting too." I held the heart-shaped locket that hung on my neck, fingered the clasp on the side. Rachel had told me that I had to fill it myself. *Fill it with something that gives you joy,* she said.

"What about Mia?" my father asked. "You're just going to leave her?" I held my breath.

"David," my mother said, so low I could barely hear. "I can't take her with me."

"You can't, or you won't?" my father asked.

The loon's call sounded again. Sharper, more frantic.

"Both," my mother said.

"You tell her," my father said. I heard his footsteps retreating down the hall, then the front door opening and shutting, and finally the sound of his truck's engine and the tires on gravel.

I waited for my mother to find me.

The sky grew dark. I heard the sounds of drawers opening and closing. The sounds of zippers. The sounds of packing. Then silence. I lay on my bed in the darkness, holding my empty locket in my hand. I must have fallen asleep, because the next thing I knew it was dawn, and there was an envelope with my name on it on the floor beside my bed. My mother's usually beautiful handwriting was cramped and shaky.

I closed my eyes, trying to find Rachel again in my dreams. Trying to hear her voice. But all I heard was the long, mournful cry of a loon echoing from across the lake. I held my breath, waiting for the reply that always came, the same mournful cry of its mate, but it never did. I lay there, listening to the single loon calling and calling.

Veronica takes me to church again on Sunday afternoon. Mostly it's the same: Kneel. Pray. Stand. Repeat. And I wonder if it's because they think God likes it that way. The sameness. But that can't be true. God must love variety. Beetles that sparkle like emeralds. Giant flowers that smell like moldy cheese. The platypus?

Then there's the wine and the bread, which I don't take, but which I also thankfully don't spill. My grandmother lights a candle before we leave, then another. And another. I stand at the back of the church, waiting. Are candles something else God needs? Or are they lit because we need something to do? Something to hold on to?

Veronica bows her head for a few moments. Then we start back to her apartment in silence. I wonder who the candles were for. One was for Rachel, for sure. But the other two? Herself, maybe? Me? I stare at the cracks in the side-walk as we walk.

I step down off the curb, and hear the car before I see it. Tires squeal and a horn sounds, too loud and too close. Veronica's hand is on my arm, yanking me back onto the sidewalk. The driver guns the car past us in a cloud of exhaust and profanity. I see my grandmother saying something to me, see her arms waving as she talks, but she sounds far away.

My skin feels clammy and my heart is racing. I sit on the edge of a planter, willing my breathing to slow. It's the smell that undoes me. The smell of burning rubber com-ing off the skid mark in front of me—dark and burnt and familiar. I close my eyes. All I can see are the lights on the dashboard of Rachel's car and then the dark road through the windshield. There's the sound of tires squealing and that same sharp smell. Then pain, like fire running through me as I'm thrown forward.

Then screaming. Two voices.

Then just one.

"Mia!" Veronica's voice pulls me free from the memory. Her hand is on my arm. "Are you okay?"

I look up at her and nod. I stand, still shaken, and take a deep breath, tasting the burnt rubber on my tongue.

"I'm okay," I say. She looks at me for a long moment, the longest she's ever looked at me. "I'm sure," I say, now as undone by her concern as the quickly disappearing memory.

Veronica nods, her face pale. She holds my arm all the way to her building and into the elevator, and I wonder who is holding up whom. She only releases my arm so she can unlock her front door.

"Go sit down," she says, leading me into the living room.

As she walks into the kitchen, I sink into a chair. I'm tired—way down in my bones tired. Veronica returns and hands me a glass of water. I take a sip.

"Better?" she asks. I nod and listen as she rants about the dangers of city drivers.

"They're no worse than the logging trucks up north," I say. My voice is still shaky.

"I suppose not," she agrees.

I think about what I remembered. It's the first time there's been more than still shots, little collections of partly developed Polaroids.

Veronica asks me again if I'm okay. I again nod yes. She narrows her eyes slightly.

"*Really,*" I say. My stomach growls. "I'm a little hungry," I admit.

Veronica is up instantly. "What can I get you?" she asks.

"Do you like pizza?" I ask.

Veronica opens her mouth to say something, and then quickly shuts it again. Her cheeks go pink. "I've never had pizza," she finally says.

I can't keep the surprise off my face. "Seriously?" I ask. She nods rather sheepishly. "We have to change that," I say, surprised at how bold I'm being with her.

"Okay," she says simply. "Let's order a pizza." She gets up and retrieves her phone. I tell her the name of the pizza place I went to.

"Do you want me to order?" I ask.

"Talk me through it," she says. "If I'm going to have a teenager in the house, I'd better figure out how to order a pizza."

When the food arrives, Veronica really gets into their *Under Thirty Minutes or It's Free* claim, letting the delivery guy know that he was one minute away from buying us dinner. I set the table while she negotiates his tip. I'm pleased to note that even a guy with a tattoo of an octopus on his neck is intimidated by Veronica. He thanks her for what must be a pretty nice tip and tells her to have a nice night.

Veronica serves both of us slices of Veggie Heaven. She uses her knife and fork to cut off the end of her triangle. I start to do the same, but she waves my utensils away. "It's perfectly okay to eat some foods with your hands," she says.

I wait as she takes a bite. She chews carefully, swallows daintily, and then dabs. "It's good," she says.

"We should do this again," I say.

"We should," she says. This makes me smile. *Look at us. Eating dinner together and smiling.* After dinner, I tell Veronica I'll clean up. She tells me she has a novel she wants to finish.

Dishes for two people take a lot less time than dishes for four. I glance at the clock. Not even seven. I pull out my phone and stare at it. One missed call, from Fig. I think about calling my father—it's been a week since he tried to call me. But instead I return Fig's call. She doesn't answer her cell. I get her voice mail; just a *leave a message and I'll give you a holler*, in a terrible faux Texas accent. I try Brunelli's. I get Grace.

"Hi, Grace," I say, my voice wavering from nerves. That woman terrifies me. "Is Fig there?" She doesn't answer, instead just barely moves the receiver away from her mouth before yelling Fig's name. I wince as her voice drills a hole into my brain. There's a thunking noise and then nothing. I wonder if the call's been dropped, but then I hear more thunking and Grace's voice, then Fig's.

"So how was church?" Fig asks.

"It was good," I say. "We had pizza."

"At church?"

"No, here. Veronica and I ordered pizza."

"Weird," she says.

Definitely a little weird. I hear Grace yelling again, then Fig's voice is muffled, like she put her hand over the receiver.

"I'm sorry, Mia," she says. "I have to go. It's family dinner night." I can almost hear her eyes rolling through the phone. "What are you doing?"

I look around at the closed door and the empty apartment. "Nothing," I say.

"Well, I'm not going to invite you to dinner," she says. "Because I like you. If I ever invite you, you know it's

because I'm mad at you." There's more yelling in the background. "Okay!" Fig yells. This time she doesn't cover the
mouthpiece, and I have to pull my phone away from my
ear. "Sorry," she says. "Listen. Call Cooper. No, wait. Don't
call him. Go see him." She rattles off an address. I pull a
Sharpie out of a drawer and write on the palm of my hand.

"What is this?" I ask.

"Just go there," she says. I can hear Grace's voice through
the phone, staccato and loud, telling Fig if she doesn't get
off the phone, she's going to—then the rest of it is muffled.
"I'll see you tomorrow," Fig says.

She hangs up before I can say goodbye. I stand there
and look at the address on my hand.

I walk over to the door into the living room, where
Veronica is reading intently. Once again, I don't have much
of an explanation for where I'm going. "I'm going for a
walk," I say, because it's the truth.

Veronica looks at me for a moment, and I can almost tell
she's pulling away from the story she's reading just enough
to talk to me. "Be back before dark," she says.

"Before dark," I repeat, but Veronica is already back in
her book. I grab my bag and a jacket from the hall closet
and head out.

Chapter Eleven

I check the address on my palm again and look up at the buildings lining the other side of the street. I followed the directions on my phone, walking through the crisscrossed streets of downtown. The whole block in front of me is filled with brick buildings that look more like they were cloned than built, but their signs couldn't be more different. There's Dharma's Holistic Healing, Ken's Computer Repair, a store named Scoops that seems to sell only spoons. There's a market on the corner with pyramids of watermelons out front that look like the softest touch might send dozens of melons rolling out into the street.

I count the buildings, stopping at a middle one that has no sign, only a blue-and-green awning and a wooden cutout of a hand pointing to the door. I take a breath and start another round of the argument I've been having with myself the whole time I've been walking.

There have been some variations, but it's something like this:

You sure you want to do this?

Maybe.

What if Cooper doesn't *want* to see you?

(silence)

What if he's busy?

(silence)

What if Fig's just setting you up?

She wouldn't do that.

No, she probably wouldn't. But what if Cooper thinks you're weird, or a freak, or ugly, or boring?

But—

What if he thinks you're damaged? What if he's just being nice because he feels sorry for you? What if he found out who you really are, what you really did?

(silence)

You sure you want to do this?

Yes.

This last part I say out loud, so loud that I startle a woman walking past. I wait for a cab to pass, then jog across the street. The sign on the door that I couldn't see from across the street says, "There. Opening Soon." From the sidewalk, I can hear music and hammering and swearing. Mostly music. I tentatively step inside. The hammering and swearing is coming from my right, but there is music in front of me. I opt for the music. I walk forward into the large room, where stacks of chairs and tables are pushed against the side walls. Ornate light fixtures blaze, revealing an antique tin ceiling.

Wood paneling covers most of the walls. Only the back wall is left open. There, Cooper is standing on a long board balanced on top of two stepladders. His back is to me and he's holding a stack of something that looks like blue playing cards. He holds one up, then another, considering them against the wall. I stand there, simply watching him. He bends and picks up another stack of colored squares and begins holding them up one by one. Finally, he pauses, holding one up longer than the others.

I tell myself I haven't told him I'm here because I don't want to startle him and make him fall off his makeshift scaffolding. But that's only partly true. I haven't said anything just in case I decide that I was right all along and I'm not actually sure I do want to do this. But I'm also just watching him. Watching how he is when he thinks he's alone. Wondering if I'm that calm, that careful, that—

"Another one of Cooper's admirers, eh?" The voice from behind me makes me jump. I turn and see a man wearing a dirty T-shirt and jeans and holding a hammer. Alarm bells start ringing in my head. Weird guy, nearly empty building, hammer. That has danger written all over it. But then I hear Cooper's voice.

"Mia?" Just my name, but the way he says it makes me feel like sticking my tongue out at the other Mia and saying "See?"

I turn toward Cooper and watch him climb down from the platform and start walking toward me. "Hey," he says. "What are you doing here?"

"I, well, Fig said . . ." My brain is working furiously, trying to put words together that make sense.

"I'm glad you stopped by," Cooper says. He looks past my shoulder. "Mia, this is Simon." I glance over at the disheveled man with the hammer. He smiles at me. "Simon owns this place."

"Hi," I say, still feeling nervous.

"Hi yourself," Simon says. "Hope I didn't scare you." I shake my head, not wanting to tell him the truth. Simon looks at the side of my face for a beat too long and seems to consider something, but then he just nods to himself. "Lot of people wandering in here." He winks at Cooper, who, I swear, blushes. "I should close the door, but the AC's not hooked up yet, and with the door shut, it's an oven." There's a familiar bump in his voice. Less an accent and more a way of speaking.

"Are you from Maine?" I ask. Simon grins and Cooper rolls his eyes.

"Good luck," Cooper whispers. I hear his words, but I also feel them on my cheek and the side of my neck. *Pull it together, Mia!*

"Born up to The County. Grew up Downeast," Simon says, his accent definitely thicker. I smile. Few people south of Portland would have any idea what he just said.

"I'm from Brunswick," I say. He squints at me. I know

I'm barely from Maine as far as he's concerned, but then he smiles and looks over at Cooper.

"You tell this one, she's welcome here anytime. Ah'yuh. Anytime." Simon nods at me one more time and walks under the archway, to the other side of the wall where he was working. Cooper is shaking his head at me.

"What?" I ask.

"Simon doesn't like anyone," Cooper says. "I mean, he barely likes me."

"I don't much like you!" Simon yells from the other side of the wall, making me laugh.

"See? But you say less than a half dozen words to him and he likes you."

"I'm a likeable person," I say. The other Mia seems sort of shocked at this, but she stays quiet.

"You are," Cooper says. I can't keep from blushing at this. "I didn't know you were from Maine," Cooper says.

I shrug. Something Rachel used to say runs through my mind. *What you don't know about me could fill the ocean.*

"Want to see something?" he asks. I follow him over to the scaffolding. There are dozens of piles of colored squares scattered all around the ladders like miniature rainbow-colored skyscrapers.

"What is all this?" I ask. Cooper picks up a stack near his foot and hands it to me. I take the first square off the stack and look at it, not sure what it is. I flip it over. On the back are a row of numbers, the words *Navajo Sunset*, and the name of a hardware store in Brooklyn.

"They're—" Cooper begins.

"Formica samples," I say.

Cooper grins. "They prefer the term *laminates*."

I sift through the pile, turning each one over as I go. There's *Orange Crush, Pumpkin, Apricot, Tangerine Whisper.* "Where did you get all these *laminate* samples?" I ask.

Cooper looks a little sheepish. "Let's just say I'm not welcome in most of the hardware stores in the tristate area." I raise my eyebrow at him. "In my defense, they are free, but I'm pretty sure you're supposed to take one or two, not forty-seven."

I put the stack of orange down and pick up a tower of pink. *Peony, Fruit Punch, Whisper of a Rose.* "They like to use the word *whisper*," I say. I look up to see Cooper watching me. I duck my head, letting my hair fall across the side of my face. When I glance back up again, Cooper is frowning a little, but not at me. At the wall.

I can see the wall better now that I'm closer and not distracted by a strange man wielding a hammer. Someone has drawn all over the wall in pencil. "Wow," I say. I have to step back to see it better. "You did this?" As soon as I say it, the other Mia smirks at me, *Duh.* But Cooper just nods.

"Simon asked me to do a mural. At first, I was just going to paint it, but then I went to this Impressionist exhibit at the Met." Cooper looks over at me. "You know how those paintings just look like a mess close up, but from a distance . . ."

I nod. When he talks about painting, about painters, his

whole face changes. He gets this faraway look in his eyes, like he's half here and half somewhere else.

"I thought instead of paint, maybe a mosaic." He looks back at me.

"It's amazing," I say, wondering if that wasn't the same thing I said about his version of *Starry Night*. I put the stack of pink tiles I'm holding back on the floor, careful to keep them from falling over.

Then Cooper looks over at me. "You want to help?" he asks.

"Yes," I say, not sure what I'm agreeing to.

"Good," he says. "I could use another artist's eye." The other Mia smirks at me. *You're just another groupie. Like Simon said: "another admirer."* Almost as if he can read my mind, Cooper looks at me. "I can trust you, right?" he asks. His voice is serious.

"Yes," I say.

"Good, because this project is top secret."

I feel a warmth in my chest that spreads up to my face, making my cheeks hot.

"You can trust me," I say.

He looks at me for a long time, then nods. "I think I can," he says. The way he says it makes me wonder if this is about more than the mural. And I wonder if he has the same feeling about me that I do about him. That I want to trust him. Maybe even *need* to trust him.

"Okay, you two," Simon yells from the doorway. "I'm not paying you to stand around."

Cooper shakes his head at him. "As far as I know, you're not paying me at all."

Simon snorts. "I bought you lunch." He digs into his pocket and drops a couple of bills on the counter. "Here. After work, take your girlfriend out for an ice cream or something."

I'm suddenly unable to look at anything but the toes of my sneakers. Why do adults always do that? I can hear Simon laughing all the way into the next room. I glance out of the corner of my eye at Cooper, but he's just sifting through a stack of brown tiles. He seems completely unfazed by what Simon just yelled across the room. Then he turns toward me.

"So, you want to get ice cream after?" Cooper asks. I can only bob my head. Maybe he didn't catch the part about the girlfriend. But then Cooper winks at me before climbing up on the scaffolding. The other Mia just stands there with her mouth open. For once, at a loss for words.

We work for about half an hour. Mostly me handing stacks of tiles up to Cooper and telling him whether *Crazy About Carrots* is a better choice than *24 Carrots*.

I call Veronica and tell her I'm going to be a tiny bit late, but I won't walk home alone. She tells me to be careful and then, just before she hangs up, tells me to have fun. Cooper and I walk over a couple of streets to a place with a giant plastic ice cream cone hanging out over the sidewalk. When we walk up to the window to order, the girl behind the counter makes a face at me, but grins at Cooper. She looks at his mouth for a moment, but it's not even close to being enough to turn her off. She actually bats her eyes at him.

"Hey there," she says. "What can I get for you?"

"You first, Mia," he says, completely ignoring the flirting. I get mint chocolate chip. Cooper gets strawberry. Apparently, I make a face when he orders his cone.

"What's wrong with strawberry?" he asks as we wait for our cones.

"It's not chocolate," I say.

"Well, technically yours isn't chocolate either," he says. "It's mint."

"With chocolate," I insist.

"What if I got strawberry *with* chocolate?" he asks.

"I would feel sorry for you." This makes him laugh. A guy brings our order to the window, and I immediately take a bite of my ice cream, leaving a divot in the front.

"Truth or dare?" Cooper asks as we start making our way back toward Veronica's.

"Dare," I say without pausing.

"A risk-taker," Cooper says. We stop and watch a flock of pigeons fighting over a discarded hot dog bun. "You have to eat your ice cream without stopping for one full minute."

"Alright," I say. I stop in the middle of the sidewalk to show that I'm serious.

Cooper looks at his watch. "Go." I start licking, but Cooper begins protesting immediately. "Eat, not lick." He looks back at his watch. "Go. Again." I start taking bites out of my ice cream until it looks like a giant green-and-brown golf ball. After only a dozen bites or so, I start to feel that pressure between my eyes.

I press my free hand to my forehead. "Ow." I close my eyes. "Brain freeze." I squint at Cooper, who looks half concerned and half amused. The pain is gone as quickly as it started, but lesson learned. "How'd I do?" I ask.

"Twenty-eight seconds." I frown. "You have to train for these things, Mia." His voice is serious, but his eyes are teasing. "You know what this means."

"What?" I ask.

"You have to answer my question." I nod, hoping my face isn't giving away what I'm thinking. "Truthfully."

"I got that part," I say, trying to make my voice lighter than I feel. Truth scares me. I start walking again, thinking that if I have to tell him the truth, I'd rather do it while in motion.

Cooper walks beside me, taking small bites from his cone. "What made you move here?" he asks.

This is an easy one. "My dad's down in Florida this summer at dive school. He works for the state of Maine doing search and rescue. Essentially, he's a water policeman," I say.

Cooper nods, and I wince inside. The very last thing I want to do is lie to Cooper. No, that's not exactly right. The last thing I want to do is tell the whole truth to Cooper. What I said isn't a lie, but it's not exactly the truth either. Or at least not all of it.

"So, you're headed home at the end of the summer?" he asks.

I don't know how to answer that. I'm not even sure I still have a home to head back to. Suddenly the ice cream seems too sweet. We turn onto Veronica's street and start making our way to her building. A guy in a suit stands on the corner playing soft jazz music on his saxophone.

"I thought I only had to answer one question," I say, trying hard to make that ache in my chest go away.

Cooper looks at me, and I have that same feeling. Like he knows me. Like he can see inside me. "Fair enough," he says, finally. "Your turn."

"Okay," I say. "Truth or dare?"

"Truth," Cooper says. He says it so quickly that it makes the ache in my chest even worse.

"When we picked up Waffles the other day and I asked if you lived in that apartment, you told me it was complicated." I pause, trying to work out what I'm trying to ask.

"I'm afraid you'll have to phrase your question in the form of a question," Cooper says. He takes another bite of his cone, but it's sort of halfhearted.

"Where do you live?" I ask.

"Sarah and I live there," he says. "Legally."

"What about actually?" I ask.

Cooper shrugs. "Most nights I crash at Sebastian's, and Sarah stays with Fig. Our grandmother is not always a very reliable guardian," he says. I wait for more, but he doesn't offer an explanation. "This is you, right?" he asks. I look up, surprised to see that we're already at Veronica's building.

"Yeah," I say. "But wait." I dip my hand into my bag and pull out my camera. "I want to take a picture."

I hand Cooper my half-eaten ice cream and aim the camera at the man with the saxophone. He's backlit against the park lights. But I don't take pictures of him. I glance over at Cooper, who is looking across the street. His face is half in shadows. I turn my camera on him and zoom in close. *Click.* I shift back to the music man just as Cooper looks over, then turn off my camera and slip it back into my bag.

"All finished?" he asks. I nod and accept my quickly melting ice cream cone from him. "I know you have to get up early," he says.

I nod, even though what I want to say is, *I'm fine. Let's just sit here and eat ice cream and listen to music and—*

"I should get going," he says. I nod again. He pauses for a moment, like he'd rather stay too, but then he turns and walks back the way we came and I'm left standing there, with melted ice cream dripping down my arm and a crazy smile on my face.

"Good evening, Miss Mia," the doorman says when I head inside.

"Definitely," I say.

Chapter Twelve

I barely have my apron on before Fig starts peppering me with questions. "You had ice cream?" Fig asks.

I swear, if she keeps wagging her eyebrows like that, she's going to make her forehead cramp up.

"Was it awesome?" she asks. We walk over to the counter, where Nonna has a pile of cinnamon roll dough waiting.

"It was okay," I say, looking intently into the mixing bowl, which is filled with brown sugar and cinnamon.

Fig turns and looks at me. "Mia Hopkins," she says. "Did you or did you not have ice cream with Cooper?"

"Did," I say.

"Are you or are you not smitten with Cooper?"

I squint at her. "Smitten?"

Fig waves her hand at me. "Crushing. Besotted. Infatuated."

"What was the question?" I ask. I use a fork to break up the clumps of brown sugar for the cinnamon roll filling.

Fig rolls her eyes at me. "Is there pining?"

"Pining?"

"You know, do you think about him? Do you try to figure out ways to see him again?" She leans toward me and lowers her voice. "Are you falling for him?"

"It's complicated," I say. And that is the truth. It's been a really long time since I've trusted anyone.

Fig flips her fingers in the air again as if waving away my words. "It's not that complicated, Mia. You're smitten with him."

I start to protest, but she just holds her hand up. "He's smitten with you."

"What?" She grins at me and her eyebrows start wagging again. "Did he tell you that?" I ask.

"No," she says. I look back down at the bowl in front of me. "But I can tell."

"How?" I ask.

She shrugs. "You remember how I told you Cooper was hard to get to know? Closed?" I nod, still looking in the bowl. "He's less so now."

"Less?" I ask.

"Since he met you," she says. "Definitely less." I use my fork to trace patterns in the sugar. Circle. Star. Heart. "Trust me," Fig says. It seems like a lot of people want me to trust them.

Nonna pushes into the kitchen and glares at Joey, who is cleaning the meat slicer.

"That better shine when you're finished!" she yells. He bobs his head and keeps working. "Who put this here?" she asks, kicking at a bucket filled with hand towels.

"Don't make eye contact," Fig whispers.

I keep stirring the sugar. "What's wrong?" I whisper.

Fig shrugs. "I'm not sure, but clearly—" Nonna steps over and looks over my shoulder, silencing Fig.

I can actually *feel* her standing there. She reaches past me and starts smashing the butter into the sugar and cinnamon to make the filling. I step back to avoid the flying ingredients and elbows.

"So, Nonna—" Fig begins.

Nonna shoots her a look, which silences her. Nonna keeps working the sugar, then moves on to the dough, rolling and flouring and punching until the whole counter is covered with a huge sheet of dough.

"Butter," she says. Fig jumps at the word, then hands her a block of butter, which Nonna drops onto the dough. "Have you talked to your mother?" At first, I'm not sure whether she means me or Fig, but then she looks at Fig.

"No," Fig says. "Why?"

Nonna starts smearing butter all over the dough. She's so aggressive that her fingers push straight through at one point. She curses. The whole kitchen goes silent, but Nonna doesn't seem to notice. She keeps buttering, and then starts sugaring.

"You talk to your mother," Nonna says, jabbing a sugary finger at Fig. She rolls the dough into a long log, pinching it shut. She grabs a big chef's knife as she says, "You talk to her or I will."

Nonna gives the dough a hard whack, cutting it clear through the middle. We stand clear as she single-handedly finishes the rolls and puts them into the pans to rise. She grabs a side towel and heads into her office, shutting the door with such force, I'm surprised the glass window doesn't break.

"Listen," Fig says to me, "you'd better head over without me." Sebastian is entered in an eating contest, which Fig swears will be fun to watch.

"What's going on?" I ask. Fig shrugs. It's not only Nonna who is acting alien-possessed. Joey has finished cleaning the meat slicer and is now smashing potatoes like they are the enemy. Grace is grinding enough coffee beans to last a year. "I can wait," I say. I'm not that anxious to go anyway.

Fig shakes her head. "Go. With my mother, there's no telling how long it's going to take to *talk* to her. I'll come over after we're through." I grab my bag from under the counter and start to pull my hair out of the ponytail I have to wear at work. Fig touches my arm. "You should leave your hair up," she says. "It looks nice that way."

I snort. "Maybe my hair looks nice when it's up, but not my face." I yank the elastic free and feel my hair fall across my cheek.

"Mia," Fig says, "how long did you notice Cooper's mouth?" I think back to the first day I met him and how I was shocked at first, but after seeing his artwork and talking to him, I simply didn't notice his mouth anymore. Fig nods like she can read what I'm thinking. "It's the same thing with you, you know."

"It's not," I say, and I don't just mean what my face looks like; it's what it represents. How my face is the outside view of the ugliness inside.

"I'm not going to lie to you, Mia," Fig says. "The first time I saw you, all I could see was that side of your face." She points to the right side. The ruined side. "But after about three minutes, I totally forgot about it. In fact, the only time I even notice it is when you point it out." I look at her. Either she's an excellent liar or else she really is telling the truth.

"It's not just this," I say, pointing to my scar.

"Then what is it?" she asks. I bite my lip and shake my head. "Listen," Fig says. "Whatever it is—you can tell me."

"Not here," I say.

Fig shakes her head, a faint smile touching her mouth. "No, here's probably not the best place." Gina comes in at that moment and freezes when she sees Fig. "We'll talk later," Fig says to me.

She turns toward Gina, who is trying to slide back through the door. "Mom," Fig says, "Nonna says we should talk. Tell me what's going on." Gina goes white, then starts crying. "Mom!" Fig says, loudly. "Stop with the theatrics. Tell me."

I'm shocked at how Fig is talking to her mom, knowing I would never consider talking to either one of my parents like that. But with Gina, it seems to do the trick, because she stops crying like she just shut off a faucet. She heads toward the office.

Fig follows her and starts to close the door behind them, but then she stops and looks at me. "We'll talk later," she repeats in a serious tone. I nod. I am definitely not about to disagree with Fig right now. Then Fig smiles. "I'll meet you when I'm done." She starts to close the door, then stops again. "Say hi to Cooper for me." She grins at me, then shuts the door.

I slip my hair elastic onto my wrist. Despite what Fig says, I'm not ready to walk around as the girl with half a face. I make my way through the front, where everyone seems frozen in place. They all talk in half-whispers, their eyes darting over to Nonna, who has reemerged from her office. Only Grace says goodbye to me as I leave. That is perhaps more disturbing than the silence from everyone else.

I slide my sunglasses on as I move onto the sidewalk, wondering what is going on in that office and why everyone is acting like someone just died.

I walk over to the park only a couple of blocks away. Having to get to work so early stinks, but at least it means I have all afternoon to myself. People crowd the sidewalk, positioned behind ribbon barriers strung between signs advertising Joe's Kosher Franks. I see Sarah standing to one side under a tree, and she waves and grins when she spots me. She doesn't say anything, only nods, when I tell her Fig is going to come by after she talks to her mom.

"Eating contests seem more like a weekend event," I say. "I mean, who wants to go back to work after horking down two dozen hot dogs?"

"No one," Sarah agrees. "But apparently there was some controversy over the last contest." I make a face, which causes her to laugh. "Seriously. Some guy was shoving hot dogs into his shirt. So they had to rerun it." She wags her head toward the front. "Come on," she says.

We weave through the crowd, trying to find an empty spot. Sarah leads us off to one side, telling me we shouldn't stand in the first few rows. "There's a lot of food that goes flying," she says. I grimace, and she nods. "I got hit in the head with a half-eaten hot wing last month."

I've never been to an eating contest, or, as Sebastian calls it, a gastronomical competition. There's a long table set up on a stage. Behind it are at least twenty people. Sebastian is way down on one end.

"How many of these has he done?" I ask, pointing toward the stage where Sebastian is listening as one of the judges reads the rules.

"A bunch," Sarah says, shrugging. "I've only been to a couple of them. The wing one and a watermelon one last summer. Fig's been to all of them, though."

A couple of women in too-tight shorts and tank tops start passing out platters of hot dogs. Sebastian stares at the mound of hot dogs placed in front of him. "He looks nervous," Sarah says.

"I would be," I say, glancing at the hundreds of people around us. "This is a big crowd."

"This is one of the pre-qualifiers for the Nathan's contest on the Fourth of July. If he makes it in, he'll be the youngest competitor ever."

"How many does he have to eat?" I ask.

"This one is a timed contest, so he just has to eat as many as he can in two minutes." I look at the mound of hot dogs in front of him, glad I don't have to eat them all.

"I could eat three," I say.

Sarah smiles. "Me too. Maybe."

I nod in agreement. I look around at the people pushing in on all sides. Two news crews have their cameras trained on the competitors. The judge steps away from the tables, and the competitors start getting antsy as a bunch of photographers step forward to take pictures. I pull out my camera too and aim it straight at Sebastian.

Once I'm confident I have a good angle, I turn to Sarah. "I didn't get to tell you last week but your song was really amazing."

"Thanks," Sarah says, blushing.

"I mean it. You should try to get it recorded."

"Maybe." Sarah looks down at the ground. "Cooper says the same thing, but I don't know." She looks at me for a moment. "That song was hard for me to write. I'm not sure I'm ready to share it with the whole world."

A man steps up to the front of the stage holding a bull-horn. "On your mark."

The competitors all lean over the table, their hands clasped behind them.

"Get set."

In the pause, the whole crowd goes silent, then a voice behind me yells, "Go Sebastian!" and everyone laughs. Sebastian tries for a smile, but he just looks vaguely ill. I look in the direction of the voice and see Cooper, who is standing on the edge of the fountain so he can see over the tops of everyone's heads.

"Go!" the announcer yells.

All the competitors fall on the piles of hot dogs. I take one close-up of Sebastian just before he bites into his first hot dog. Then I take several others, thinking Fig might want to see them. I watch, horrified, as one guy shoves four hot dogs into his mouth at once. Sarah was right; bits of bun and chunks of hot dogs are flying all over anyone within ten feet of the table. I peek at the hands of a big clock set off to one side, which spin as the two minutes tick off.

I watch Sebastian down hot dog after hot dog. He isn't the fastest eater, but he seems to be one of the steadier. I watch as several people step back from the table with their hands up in defeat. I feel a hand on my arm and I jump and look back. Cooper.

"Hey," he says, smiling at me. "I didn't mean to scare you." He stands behind me. I try to concentrate on the clock, on the rapidly disappearing hot dogs, on Sebastian, who has motioned for another platter, but all I can focus on is Cooper's hand still on my arm. The weight of it. The warmth of it. I try to tell my heart to stop beating so fast, but it won't listen.

The announcer starts counting down from ten. Sebastian crams three hot dogs into his mouth at once.

"Ew," Sarah says, cringing and looking over at me. She looks at Cooper's hand on my arm and then back at my face. I can't read her expression.

The announcer yells for competitors to stop eating. Sarah looks at me for a second longer, then at the table up front. "Whatever's in his mouth still counts," Sarah says.

"As long as he can keep it down," Cooper says. I follow his gaze to where a man is bent over the trash can.

"I could have gone the rest of my life without seeing that," I say, making both Sarah and Cooper laugh. We wait while the judges count hot dogs with gloved hands.

"Partials don't count," Cooper says. One of the tank top girls follows along behind the judge, writing on a clipboard. We have to wait a long time while they count through all of the uneaten hot dogs.

"Watermelons were faster," Sarah says.

"How many watermelons did Sebastian eat?" I ask, thinking two, tops.

"Eleven," Sarah says. She laughs at the look on my face. "That contest was awful. It wasn't timed, so they just had to eat until they were full or they gave up."

"Or they threw up," Cooper says, making a face.

"Sebastian won. The next closest person was six."

"So why did he eat so many?" I ask.

"He said that the level of competition was not going to influence his individual performance," Cooper says.

Sarah laughs. "What he actually said was that just because everyone else was a bunch of wimpy babies didn't mean he had to be."

"Same thing," Cooper says. He smiles at me, making my heart race even faster. I can almost feel it clanking against the inside of my rib cage. He looks at me for a moment longer, making me wonder what color laminate matches his eyes. Probably something like *Gilded Pesto* or *Sunlit Pines*.

The judge walks over to the microphone and holds up his clipboard. He clears his throat, and the microphone screeches, making me wince. "We have the results of the Seventh-Annual Lower East Side Hot Dog Eating Contest." He pauses dramatically. "But before I announce the winner, I'd like to thank our sponsors." The crowd around us groans. He rattles off a list of businesses, including, oddly enough, Weight Watchers. Brunelli's is one of the sponsors too.

"Get on with it!" someone yells from the back, drawing applause from everyone.

The judge clears his throat again. "In third place, Mark Sacovich." There's a smattering of applause as Mark walks across the stage. I note that he looks a bit green. Second place goes to a man in overalls and a camouflaged base-ball cap.

"And in first place . . ." The judge pauses just long

enough to make everyone stop talking. "Our youngest competitor . . ." Cooper starts whistling immediately. "Sebastian
Simmons!"

Sebastian runs onto the stage and accepts a trophy with
a huge gold hot dog on the top. He also gets a certificate
that the judge explains gives him a spot in the Nathan's
Famous International Hot Dog Eating Contest in July.

The emcee keeps talking, listing other opportunities to
qualify and thanking more people, but I don't hear any of
it because Fig has arrived and she looks terrible. Her eyes
are swollen and her cheeks are still wet, and she's out of
breath like she ran all the way here from the deli. She says
something to Sarah, who covers her mouth and shakes her
head, then immediately puts her arms around Fig. Cooper
steps around me and leans toward Sarah, who says something to him. He frowns and looks toward the stage, where
Sebastian is still standing, holding up his trophy while photographers take his picture.

Cooper manages to catch his eye. Sebastian looks at
him briefly, then at Fig, who is leaning against Sarah, her
shoulders shaking with silent tears. Sebastian jumps down
from the stage amidst protests from the reporters, pushing
through the crowd until he reaches Fig. He puts his hand
on her shoulder while Cooper says something to him. Fig
looks at him, her cheeks streaked with tears, until he pulls
her to him. I stand there just watching, my hands hanging
at my sides. Cooper looks at me for a moment, then closes
his eyes and takes a deep breath.

"We should go," he says. It's clear from whom he's looking at that he doesn't mean me. Fig just bobs her head slightly and Sebastian keeps his arm around her, steering her through the crowd.

Sarah looks back at me for a moment, hesitating. "Sorry," she mouths before following.

Cooper is the last to leave. "I'll call you later," he says. Then he turns and pushes through the crowd to follow Sarah, who is getting swallowed up in all the people.

I stand there, not sure what to do. I notice there's a circle around me that no one seems able or willing to cross. Like my own bubble. My own personal space. Protected, but isolated. And more alone than ever.

Chapter Thirteen

Our neighbor, Peanut Gardner, found the dead loon, but it was my dad who had to fish it out of the lake.

"Stupid thing got himself tangled up in some fishing line," Dad told me when I saw him carrying the loon out to his truck. He carried it by its feet, its long neck hanging down toward the ground. He placed it on a tarp on the bed of his truck and covered it with another tarp. "Just going to head up to Pumpkin Ridge to dispose of it. Don't want the smell to draw the bears." I stood on the porch, my arms wrapped around myself, trying to stop shivering. It wasn't the cold—the weather was unseasonably warm for May. It was the remaining loon calling from across the lake.

They mate for life. I remember my mother telling Rachel and me that when we were young. That night, after my father went to sleep, I sat on the deck, listening as I had ever since my mother left. Listening to the loon call again and again. Every night, I sat out there, listening. The long, mournful sound would echo across the lake and raise goose bumps on my arms.

But one night I sat until all the color had faded from the sky, until the bats stopped swooping toward the water trying to catch their fill of mosquitoes. I sat there long after my father came out to tuck a blanket around me, pausing for a moment with his hand on my shoulder before stepping back inside and pulling the screen door shut behind him. I sat there until I could see my breath, and the only noises were the sounds of the leaves rustling in the wind and the distant sound of a dog barking. But no call ever came. I'm not sure which was worse: the sorrowful calls or the silence. As long as she was calling, she had hope. The silence was heavy with despair.

I check my phone every few minutes, pulling it out of the pocket of my jeans so many times that I'm surprised I haven't worn a hole in them. I feel restless, just walking from one end of the apartment to the other. My grandmother left me a note saying she was at some meeting at the MoMA and not to expect her back until after dinner.

I fix myself a bowl of oatmeal and eat it over the sink, half wishing Veronica were here to see this. I can't even imagine how many rules I'm breaking. Eating standing up. Clanking my spoon against my bowl. Slurping my milk. Chewing with my mouth open. Finally, the phone does ring, but it's not my cell. It's my grandmother's landline. I pick it up on the second ring, thinking maybe it's Fig or Cooper or someone who can tell me what's going on, but it's not any of them. It's my dad.

"Oh," Dad says. "Hey there." From his voice, it's clear that he didn't expect me to answer. He clears his throat. "I thought you'd be . . ." And he pauses, probably because he has no idea what I might be doing.

I don't say anything. The silence stretches for so long that he asks me if I'm still there.

"Yes," I say. Another silence.

Then, "How are you doing?" He sounds sincere, and it makes my heart ache, but I force myself to remain cold. I've been tricked before. First, they hook you, then they start reeling you in. Then, bam, they cut the line.

"Fine," I say after another long pause.

"I miss you, Mia."

I close my eyes. Everything in me wants to tell him that I miss him too, but I don't. Because I'm not sure if the father I miss even exists anymore. I miss the dad I had before. The dad who would drop everything to have snowball fights with us. The dad who would wake me up at midnight to go out onto the deck and watch the northern lights.

I don't miss the dad who dropped me off at the train station. The one who's forgotten how to hug or smile or even look at me.

"I like your photos," I say instead.

"Do you?" His voice is so pleased, it makes me feel mean and small for holding out on him. We don't say anything for several moments, and I wonder if he's considering the fork in the conversation ahead of us. *Go right for more chit-chat or left for a real conversation.*

"Is Veronica around?" he finally asks, taking the road on the right.

"No," I say, staring a hole in the wall above the sofa.

My dad clears his throat, possibly reconsidering his route. "I talked to your mom," he says.

This gets my attention. "I thought she wasn't able to talk for a while," I say.

"Well, they've made extra allowances for our *special situation*," Dad says. I roll my eyes. *Special situation* makes it sound a lot nicer than a wife and mother taking off and going all the way across the country to join a convent. Seriously. My mother is now a nun.

"What did she say?" I ask, despite my resolve not to engage my father too much.

"She said she was doing well. Said she talked to you." I shake my head. More like talked *at* me. "She said she was worried about you."

I close my eyes. "She has a funny way of showing it," I say.

The cold anger in my voice surprises both of us into silence. I wait for the excuse he tried to give me after my mom left. *She just needs some time.* I believed that right up until the point I dug her attorney's letter out of the trash. The one in which she stated that she was giving up not only custody to my dad, but all her parental rights. There it was in black and white. My mother officially and legally abandoned me.

I left the letter on the center of my father's desk. He knew I saw it, but neither of us ever talked about it.

My father clears his throat again. "Veronica says you have a job and some friends."

My cheeks get hot. I hate that they talked about me, like I'm some sort of weird science experiment they're keeping record of.

I hear an engine starting up on my father's end of the phone. "When are you coming back, Dad?" I ask.

"What's that?" he says. He's yelling because he can't hear me, but I can hear him fine. I have to hold the phone away from my ear.

"Nothing," I say. I'm not going to repeat that question.

"Listen, Mia-bird," he says, using an old nickname. I wince. "I'll call you in a few days." He's still shouting, and now I am having trouble hearing him over the roar of the engine. "I want to—" A loud noise drowns out whatever he said.

The call starts breaking up. "I have to go," he says. "I—"

And the call is gone. I'd like to imagine that he was going to say he loved me, but I don't let myself go very far down that road. Rachel's death created a black hole that sucked everything into it. Love was one of the things that got lost.

I stare at the phone in my hand until it starts beeping, reminding me to hang up. I lean against the same wall I was trying to stare a hole into and close my eyes. The thing I hate most about all of this is that I have no right to say anything. I have no right to complain. I did this to myself. I did it to all of us.

Because of me, my sister is dead and my mother is gone and my father is lost.

It's all my fault.

I finally turned my phone off around one in the morning. When I turn it back on as I walk to the deli only three hours later, there are still no missed calls.

Nonna greets me with the longest list yet. I frown when I see rugelach, black and whites, and spice drops *again*.

"What's going on, Mia?" Nonna asks. Nothing gets by her.

"Nothing," I say. "I'm sorry." I start to tie on my apron.

"You're upset," she says. "Talk to me."

"It's nothing. I'm just . . ."

Nonna nods encouragingly, but I can't finish. Sometimes when there's too much to say, I can't say anything.

Nonna plucks the list from my hands, rips it in half, and drops the pieces into the trash. "Let's make something new," she says.

"What?" I ask.

"You tell me," she says. I start to shrug, but she's not going to let me off the hook. "Tell me about something from when you were little."

I shake my head. "I don't know," I say.

"Close your eyes," she says.

I take a peek around. We're the only ones in the kitchen. At least there won't be a bunch of witnesses to this impromptu therapy session. I nod and close my eyes.

"You and your mother are in the kitchen. What are you making?" As she talks, I can actually see my mother standing in tree pose at our kitchen island. She always did yoga balance postures while she was cooking. She's using an ice cream scoop to place balls of chocolate dough onto a cookie sheet. A stand mixer filled with fluffy white frosting whirls beside her. I feel myself smile.

"Whoopie pies," I say, opening my eyes. Nonna is grinning at me. "I want to make whoopie pies."

When the morning rush is over, Nonna finds me helping Grace restock the pastry baskets. She waves a piece of paper in her hand and motions for me to follow her into the kitchen. She's standing at one of the work tables, surrounded by a sea of ingredients. A huge tin of cocoa powder, a gallon jug of vanilla, and the biggest can of marshmallow fluff I've ever seen join the ever-present bins of flour and sugar. I walk over to stand next to Nonna.

"What do you think?" Nonna asks. She moves the sheet of paper in front of me. *Downeast Whoopie Pies* is written across the top in her loopy handwriting. "Does this look right?"

I scan the list. "I think so," I say, "but we never used whipped cream." She grabs her pen and scratches off whipped cream from the ingredient list. "But the rest looks right," I say.

"Just tell me what to do," Nonna says. It's awkward at first, directing Nonna in her own kitchen, but she doesn't seem to mind even when I adjust the filling recipe when it comes out too soft. We're pulling the baked cookie-cakes out of the oven in no time and lining them up on the cooling racks to be filled.

Joey comes in for his usual cinnamon roll, but when he sees what we're doing, he changes his mind. I quickly fill one of the whoopie pies and hand it to him. He takes a huge bite.

"Mia, you're my new favorite cousin," he says around a mouthful of marshmallow filling. He heads out to the front, clutching the rest of his whoopie pie.

Within moments, Nonna and I are surrounded by half of the family wanting to try "Mia's Creation." We go through a whole panful just feeding them.

"I think they're a hit," Nonna says, winking at me.

Warmth floods me. It's been a long time since I felt like I could do anything other than take up space in the world.

"Okay, everyone," Nonna says, clapping her hands. "Back to work." She helps me finish assembling the whoopie pies, then she hands me the *new* list. The rugelach and black and whites are gone, but there are at least ten more things added to the list to take their places.

Fig arrives just as I'm hauling flats of strawberries out of the cooler. She looks as bad as she did yesterday. Maybe worse.

"Hey," she says, coming up to me.

"Hey," I say back.

I decided last night that if she had wanted to talk to me, she would have. I'm not going to push. Some part of me, a part that I'm ashamed of, is simply angry. I mean, I haven't known her or her friends that long, but for them to just leave me standing there with an *I'll call you* tossed in my direction hurt. And then no one even called. I carefully pour the strawberries into a colander and take them to the sink to wash. Fig follows me across the kitchen.

"I'm sorry I didn't call you," Fig says, as if reading my mind.

"It's fine," I say. I start slicing the tops off strawberries before dropping them into the giant pot Nonna left out for me.

"I told Cooper I'd call you," she says.

I stop mid slice. I realize that's what I'm mostly mad at. Not that Fig didn't call. She was a wreck. But that Cooper didn't after promising he would. I'm sick of people dropping me like I'm expendable.

"I meant to, and then . . ."

I glance over at her. She has her eyes closed, and I can tell she's trying to force herself not to cry.

"Listen," I say, "it's fine."

But Fig won't let it go. "It's not fine, Mia." She puts her

hand on my arm. I look at it, realizing this is the second time in two days that someone has touched me. Not because they felt bad for me or because they had to. Just because. I look up at Fig's face and see that she's actually crying now. I stand there feeling helpless while she grabs one of the towels stacked on the counter and wipes her face with it.

She takes a deep breath. "My father is a drunk." She rolls her eyes and half smiles. "I mean, my father is an alcoholic. That's what we're supposed to say. But it's the same thing. Just a nicer name."

I'm confused. "So, you just found this out?" I ask.

Fig shakes her head. "No."

"Then what happened?" Now I'm really confused.

"Yesterday my mom told Nonna that she and my father have been talking and that they want to try it again."

"Try what?" I ask, feeling like my brain is wearing a sweater.

"Try living together again. Reconciling." She looks at me. "My mom told me he's changed." Fig rolls her eyes. "She's told me that before."

She holds up her right arm, and I can see a thin, pink line running from her wrist to just under her elbow. It's the first time I've seen it, as Fig usually keeps her arms covered with long sleeves or with her self-made Sharpie tattoos. "Last time he came home, he did this. Broke my arm in two places."

"Then why is he . . ." I don't know how to finish.

"Still alive?" Fig asks, smiling grimly.

"I was thinking more like not in jail," I say.

"My mom told the police it was an accident," Fig says in a flat tone. I widen my eyes, making her nod. "Exactly." Fig takes a deep breath. "I told my mom if Frank comes home, I'm gone."

"What does your family think?"

"My family's never met Frank. Mom met him when she moved to Vegas." Fig smiles at the look on my face. "Short version. Mom took off when she was eighteen. Lied about her age. Worked as a cocktail waitress in some seedy casino. Met Frank. Had me. She says he was different when I was little." Fig raises her brows. "I can't remember Frank ever being different. The only Frank I know is drunk and violent."

"Does he ever try to talk to you?" I ask.

Fig laughs. "No way. One time he tried, and I just started screeching into the phone."

"Screeching?" I ask.

"Yeah," Fig says. "You know, like a barn owl?"

She makes a hideous, high-piercing noise that causes me to jump. Joey looks into the kitchen and then backs out again, shaking his head.

"Let's just say he doesn't try to call me anymore. But he does write all the time. Usually a bunch of crap about how sorry he is and how he's changed." Fig shakes her head. "Changed. Yeah, right."

I think of the folded piece of paper she had hidden in her pocket and wonder if that was one of Frank's letters.

"When did you move here?" I ask.

"Last year," she says. I'm surprised by this. "I thought when we moved, we left Frank behind." Fig frowns. "Guess I was wrong."

"But Cooper and Sebastian and Sarah seem like they've known you forever." I think of how close all four of them seem to be.

"We all met in this group over at the rec center." She pauses. "Nonna made me go. She thought it would help if I talked about everything." Fig sighs. "She was right. As usual."

She starts to tell me more, and then checks herself. "I can't tell you. I mean, I can tell you about me, but I can't tell you about them." I nod, feeling more outside of everything than ever.

"So what now?" I ask.

Fig shrugs. "My mom promised she wouldn't do anything for *the time being,* whatever that means. But I think she's sort of freaked out that now the whole family knows." She fidgets with the towel that is still in her hand. "I'm hopeful. I mean, Nonna already told me that no matter what, I have a place with her."

"Hopeful is good," I say.

Fig takes a deep breath. "So, that's what's going on with me," she says, making a face. "If you're going to make a break for it, this is your chance."

I shake my head. What Fig is going through matches what I was starting to believe. Deep down, everyone has something ugly or dark or painful. Maybe all we need to do is talk about all of it.

"Okay," she says. "Don't say I didn't warn you." She wipes her face one more time before tossing the towel at the laundry bag. "And you thought I was all normal," she says.

"I didn't think you were *that* normal," I say, smiling. She smiles back. I try to keep the mood light and tell her about the whoopie pies while she helps me slice up the remaining strawberries.

"Wow, Mia," Fig says. "That's huge. Nonna doesn't let anyone mess with the menu. I've gotta try one."

She hurries out front. I hear some raised voices, then she slams back into the kitchen with a whoopie pie cradled in her hands. "Last one!" she says.

Joey follows her in, claiming he had dibs, but he's too late. Fig's already taken a bite.

"Yum," she says. She breaks off the untouched half and hands it to Joey, who eats it in two bites. He offers her a fist bump and heads back to the front. Fig finishes her whoopie pie while I add the sugar to the berries and put the pot on the stovetop. We take turns stirring the mixture to make sure it doesn't burn.

"Don't think I've forgotten," Fig says. She looks hard at me. "We're going to have that talk." And I wonder what that talk will be—my family, my secrets, my missing memories, Cooper?

I don't say anything. I just nod and keep stirring, watching the strawberry mixture go around and around.

My phone vibrates in my pocket. I hand Fig the spoon, then I hold my phone up. Cooper.

I show it to Fig, who grins. "See?" she says. "Smitten."

I read the text he sent.

Meet me when you're free. Come alone.

I can't figure out whether my stomach feels funny because of the text or because of what Fig told me or because I feel like a fraud. Fig is standing there grinning at me, asking if I want to run out the back. If I actually did tell her about me, I'm pretty sure she would be the one to take off. The longer I'm here, and the more everyone tells me and trusts me, the falser I feel. Some part of me really does wish I could take off. But the selfish part of me, maybe the hopeful part of me, wants to stay.

Besides . . . where would I go?

Chapter Fourteen

Fig pushes me out the door about half an hour after Cooper texts. She tells me that love trumps strawberry jam every time. I practically skip all the way over to Simon's place. The watermelons at the corner store are gone, replaced by flats of blueberries. I pause in front of There, listening to the music and the whine of a saw blade filtering out into the street. Cooper and my dad have the same taste in music—blues and reggae swirled together with some old jazz. Blueberries and Miles Davis are making me homesick, but in a good way. A reminder that not everything is gone.

It's Simon's laughter that finally draws me inside. He walks past me as I enter, muttering about difficult creative types. His mouth tilts in a half frown. "Maybe you can light a fire under that boyfriend of yours." He smiles slightly, letting me know he's just being grumpy. He disappears into the next room, and I hear the saw blade start up again.

Cooper is sorting tiles when I walk into the main room. "Hey," he says when he sees me. As he walks my way, I can't stop looking at his eyes. *Sunlight on Clover* maybe, or *Greensleeves.*

"I want to show you something," Cooper says.

He leads me to a white line chalked on the floor about fifteen feet from the mural. We stand and look at the wall for a long moment. The giant maple tree bisecting the mural looks like it's actually growing up from the wooden floor and supporting the tin ceiling. Dozens of tiles in different shades of brown hint at bark and shadows, giving it life.

"I've been thinking a lot about you," Cooper says. My heart skips when he says this. *Cooper has been thinking a lot about me!* "I think you should do the ocean." He points to the right side of the mural where the rocks fall off into the water.

My heart slows down. *He was thinking of you as an artist,* the other Mia says. I tell her to be quiet and take the brush Cooper hands me. He tells me the plan is to mount the laminate samples where we want them, and then Simon is going to come in with his sprayer and cover the whole thing with a coating of plastic.

"Make sure they're where you want them," Simon yells from the other room. "Once I spray them, they're stuck forever."

Cooper looks over at me. "Or at least until this place goes under and someone else takes it over."

"I heard that!" Simon yells, making Cooper laugh.

"What kind of place is this?" I ask. The name, There, tells me nothing.

Cooper smiles at me. "Simon owns another place uptown. It's called Here."

"Here and There," I say. "Clever."

"Thank you!" Simon calls, and then I hear something fall to the floor followed by a lot of cursing. "I'm okay!" Simon says, but there's more cursing.

"Anyway," I say, taking a box of blue samples from Cooper, "what is this place?"

Cooper studies me for a moment, then shakes his head. "I want it to be a surprise," he says.

"Couldn't I just look up Here online or even go there and see?"

"Well, you could. But Here and There aren't the same."

"Yeah," I say. "I get that."

"Also," Cooper says, as if making a bigger point, "it's a surprise."

When I'm with Cooper, I can almost forget everything, but then something always reminds me. Occasionally it's a little thing. A laugh or a song or sometimes just a word. I can hear Rachel's voice in my head. *It's a surprise, Mia-bird.* She told me to close my eyes when she put the locket around my neck. I can feel the weight of it against my chest. Something in my face must change, because Cooper stops smiling.

"You don't like surprises," he says.

I take a deep breath. "Is it a good surprise?"

"It is." He picks up a box of brown tiles and carries it to the other end of the mural. "Trust me."

I want to tell him I'm trying to, but I just bend and start sorting through the box of blues, looking for the perfect ones to match the picture in my head. *Cadet Blue, Washed Denim, Aquamarine, Seaside Holiday, Blue Like Jazz.*

Hours go by, and it still looks like we've done nothing. Simon tells us as much.

"We're still in the planning stage," Cooper says.

"Well, get to the *doing* stage," Simon says, pointing his hammer at us. I look at the floor, at all the tiles I've sorted. It's tricky finding the right blue. I don't know how anyone chooses what color to use in their kitchen. There are at least eleven different shades of aquamarine and another four of azure.

"You'd think they'd have some sort of standard," I grumble, putting a sample of *Navy* in with the ones that are called *Midnight*, because to me they look like the same shade. Cooper is smiling at me. "What?" I ask.

"You're funny," he says.

I glare at him. "How am I funny?"

This makes him laugh. "You're just so grouchy."

I sit back on my heels and look at him. "Is it too much to ask"—I hold up a laminate sample—"for Standard Hardware and"—I hold up another sample—"Industrial Enterprises to agree on one shade and call it periwinkle?" I drop the two samples. "So far I've found at least five different samples with five different names that all look like the exact same color."

Cooper is nodding, trying to make his face match my consternation, but he's not succeeding.

"I'm serious," I say.

Cooper holds up his palm. "I know," he says. My phone vibrates and I take it out.

"Hello?" I say without checking who it is.

"Mia?" It's Veronica. "Are you all right?"

"Yeah," I say. "Why?" I check the screen on my phone and wince. Almost seven thirty. "I'm sorry," I say, standing up. "I lost track of time and—"

"When can I expect you?" she interrupts.

I glance over at Cooper, who is busy sorting browns and grays for the rocks. "I'll be there in fifteen minutes." I start to say goodbye, but then I blurt out what I'm thinking before I lose my nerve. "Is there enough food for three?" I ask.

Cooper looks over at me, brows raised.

There's a long pause. I can almost feel my grandmother thinking. "Yes," she says. "We can make do."

"Thanks," I say. "We'll be there in fifteen minutes."

"Tell the young man I'm looking forward to meeting him," she says. I raise my eyebrows. I didn't say who I was bringing with me. "Goodbye, Mia." The line clicks.

"Bye," I say. Cooper is frowning at me. My heart starts thumping. "You don't have to come to dinner—I mean, only if you want to."

"I want to. I just hoped to be a little . . ." He pauses and looks down at his paint-stained jeans and his faded blue T-shirt. "Cleaner," he finishes.

I want to tell him that he looks great. Better than great. Perfect. But all I say is, "You look fine."

He narrows his eyes at me. "Okay, I'll come, but on one condition."

"What?"

"No," he says. "Just say yes."

"Not until I know the condition," I say, but he just shakes his head. I sigh. "Fine. Yes."

Cooper smiles. He walks over and switches off the music. I follow him over to the doorway. "Simon! We're taking off," he yells.

"Have fun at dinner," Simon yells back. I swear, Simon has better ears than Fig. "Coop, watch your manners."

Cooper rolls his eyes. Unfortunately, for someone about to have dinner with Veronica, that is excellent advice.

Veronica is thrown for about half a beat when she first meets Cooper. At first, I think it's because of the way he's dressed. I mean, neither of us is clean. But then I realize it's his mouth. And more than that, I realize I don't even notice it any longer.

"How do you do?" Veronica asks, extending her hand.

"It's good to meet you," Cooper says.

"Likewise," Veronica says. And it's literally the first time I've ever heard anyone use that word without a jokey British accent. "Do come in."

I would hardly call what we have for dinner "making do," as my grandmother put it. And throughout the meal Cooper is, well, perfect. His manners are far better than mine, which, much to my embarrassment, Veronica points out. Cooper makes big eyes at me when she's in the kitchen getting him another piece of pie.

"I love pie," he says. I raise my eyebrow. He blots his mouth with his napkin, making me narrow my eyes at him.

"Here you are, Cooper," Veronica says, setting another gargantuan piece of peach pie on the table in front of him.

"This is really amazing, Ms. Thompson," he says. She smiles at him, making me narrow my eyes at her too. He takes a bite and places his fork back on his plate. I have to will my eyes not to roll. That is one of Veronica's biggest issues with me. I hear her echoing in my head. *Replace your utensils back on your plate between bites. Don't hold them like some kind of Neanderthal.*

"So, Cooper, where do you go to school?"

"Franklin Academy," he says.

She nods approvingly. "I understand they have an excellent art program."

This leads into Cooper telling her about Art Attack and her telling him about how she is training to be a docent at the MoMA. "The training is very rigorous," she says. "You wouldn't believe the things we have to memorize."

Cooper nods. "I have a friend who is working there in the Restoration Department this summer. Just as an apprentice, of course." My grandmother nods. "Maybe you know him. Sebastian Simmons?"

Veronica nods again, and I shake my head. Somehow, in two minutes, they've gotten to know each other better than I know either of them. I start clearing the table while they continue to talk about past exhibits and the upcoming Masters show the MoMA is having.

I run water over the plates before stacking them inside the dishwasher. By the time I walk back to clear the last few items, Veronica is laughing so hard she's crying. I look questioningly at Cooper, but he just smiles at me. I take his plate—which I note is empty of pie—and his glass and finish the dishes. When I return this time, Veronica has a photo album out and is showing Cooper photos of our house in Maine.

"It's beautiful," Cooper says. He looks over at me, but I look away. She quickly flips past a picture of two little girls dressed up as ballerinas, holding hands. Me and Rachel. I didn't even know she had any pictures of my life. I'm not ready to share all of this.

"Listen," I say, "I have to get up really early." It's true, but I know I'm being outrageously rude. Veronica gives me a look that says she knows it as well. Cooper just stares at me, surprised, making me feel like complete garbage.

"I should go too," he says. "Thank you for dinner, Ms. Thompson. It was delicious."

"You're welcome here anytime," she says, closing the

album. She gives me a look that makes it clear my attitude is, in fact, not welcome. "Mia, why don't you walk him to the elevator?" It's not a request.

I lead Cooper out of the apartment, and then wait in the hall with him for the elevator to come. We stand there, not saying anything. I try to think of something, but all I have is embarrassment and fear and a pinch of anger. Cooper apparently can't think of anything to say either, so we remain in silence, watching the elevator move at a glacial speed from floor to floor. It stops on the second floor for a painfully long time.

"You agreed to one condition when I said I'd come to dinner," Cooper says.

I frown and look at the floor. "Are you going to tell me what it is?" I ask.

"Not yet," Cooper says. "But soon." The elevator doors open and he steps inside. He holds the doors open and looks at me. "You won't ever know if the bridge will hold you unless you step out on it."

"Is that some sort of ancient Chinese wisdom?" I ask, confused.

Cooper shakes his head and smiles, but it's a sad smile. "Just something I've learned over the past couple of years."

"But what if you step out on it and the bridge breaks?" I ask.

Cooper looks past me, as if remembering something or trying to figure something out, then he looks back at me. "I guess you have to pick a strong bridge."

I start to ask how you can tell if a bridge is strong, but the elevator doors start beeping, which they do when you hold them open for too long.

"I should go," Cooper says. "See you tomorrow." He lifts a hand in a sort of non-waving wave and the doors close.

"See you," I say to the empty hall.

I watch the numbers light up as the elevator heads down to the lobby. Sometimes I really do wish someone could see me. See me for what I really am. But like Cooper says, you have to choose strong bridges. I haven't had much luck in that area. All of my bridges have collapsed. My mom, my old friends, my dad. Not one bridge could hold my weight. My mom left, my friends drifted away when I had to stop going to school, and my dad simply faded. I take a deep breath and steel myself before I walk back to the apartment.

As I open the door and step inside, I wonder what kind of bridge my grandmother is. I'd like to believe she's a strong one, but I just can't tell.

Chapter Fifteen

The dreams keep building. Layering sounds and images. I'm driving. Rachel is passed out in the passengers seat. It's raining and dark and the fog is rolling in off the blueberry barrens in thick waves. I keep looking over to the side to make sure Rachel is still breathing. She's so pale and her breathing is shallow, like she can't quite catch her breath. I take the turns slowly, winding along the coast toward home. Our headlights barely illuminate the yellow line bisecting the road. Suddenly there's a shape on the road. Big. A moose or a huge buck. I can't tell. I pull the wheel hard to the left, but it isn't enough. I feel the impact. See the antlers rushing at me across the hood. Definitely antlers. A buck. I look over at Rachel. She's still there, slumped against the door, but something's wrong with her neck. Then my vision goes dark and the screaming begins. But I'm not sure if it's me or Rachel.

Suddenly, everything shifts and I'm sitting up in bed and still screaming, and Veronica is pushing open the door. She's beside me, touching my hair and letting me fall against her.

"It's okay," she whispers.

"It's not," I say, my voice breaking. "Rachel's dead and it's all my fault."

Veronica pulls me away from her. "Look at me." Her voice is hard, forcing my gaze upward. "It's not your fault." I start to say something, but she talks over me. "Mia, it was an accident. A terrible accident."

"Why did she have to die? Why not me?"

She pulls me against her chest again. "I lost one grand-daughter that night. I'm glad I didn't lose two."

She doesn't say anything more, just keeps stroking my hair. I must fall asleep, because the next thing I know, the alarm on my phone is going off. I fumble for my phone, wondering if even the part about Veronica is a dream, but my bedroom door has been left ajar. When I step out into the hall, I note that Veronica's is left open a tiny bit too.

Every day, right after I finish at Brunelli's, I head over to Simon's. Joey, who's oddly observant for someone with headphones constantly glued in his ears, seems to know

I'm meeting someone, because the lunch bag he hands me on the way out contains two sodas, two sandwiches, and two giant cookies. Fig keeps pressing me for details, but I tell her it's a secret. She keeps pressing me for the *talk* too, but I tell her soon.

One Thursday, Cooper tells me we should call it quits for the day when we finish the maple tree, but it's the power outage that actually decides things. Simon curses as his saw dies and the lights flicker twice before going out. It's pitch dark inside the building because all the windows are covered with brown paper. Simon told me it was to keep things a surprise. Cooper told me it was because he doesn't want anyone from the city peering in and seeing that he's breaking about two dozen building codes.

We walk toward the door, a bright rectangle against the darkened room. Simon is already on the sidewalk, yelling at a guy in a hardhat who's standing in a cherry picker and holding a length of cable. The guy yells right back. Soon there are half a dozen people yelling at each other.

"Let's get out of here," Cooper says. He ducks back inside and comes out with my bag and his backpack. "Simon!" Cooper yells. "We're taking off!" Simon barely acknowledges him before he starts yelling at the workman again. I follow Cooper toward the end of the block and away from the rapidly growing crowd that is either actively yelling at the worker or just enjoying the show.

"Where to?" I ask.

"It's time for you to pay up," Cooper says.

"I don't know what you're talking about," I say, feigning innocence.

Cooper rolls his eyes. "Let me refresh your memory. You asked me to have dinner with your grandmother—"

"Which you enjoyed," I point out, choosing to ignore the rudeness on my part at the end of the evening.

"Which I enjoyed. But I believe I offered one stipulation to the acceptance of the invitation." It's my turn to roll my eyes. "In other words, you promised to do something, no questions asked."

I nod warily. Cooper directs me toward the stairs leading down to the subway. He digs in his pocket and pulls out his subway pass, and then instructs me to give him mine, which I find in my bag and hand to him.

"Where are we going?" I ask.

"Zip it," Cooper says. "No questions."

I look at the giant map on the wall. Dozens of lines crisscross the city. There's no way of guessing where we're headed.

"At least tell me which train we're taking," I say.

"What is it about *no questions* that you don't understand?" he teases.

He leads me down the steps and through the turnstiles. The train pulls in, sending swirling dust into the air. A screech of brakes and a warning tone, then the doors slide open. Suddenly there are people pressing against me on all sides.

"Hold on tight," Cooper says. He takes my hand in his and pulls me forward.

"So, this place you're taking me to—" I try, but Cooper

only shakes his head at me and leads me to a seat. I sit and lean back, making a frustrated noise in my throat.

"Did you just growl at me?" Cooper asks.

"Maybe," I retort.

Now that we're moving, I allow myself a small moment of freaking out about Cooper holding my hand. The train bumps us into each other as we go, making both of us laugh. It's a long ride, but watching the people keeps us busy. There's a man with seven lip rings and full sleeves of tattoos, and a woman holding a birdcage with a stuffed parrot inside. When the doors slide open at one stop, the car fills with reggae music. Another stop features a violinist and an opera singer vying for an audience.

A garbled message announces the next stop.

"This is us," Cooper says. The train slows and Cooper stands, pulling me up with him. We step off the train and toward the gates leading out of the station.

"I smell water," I say.

Cooper laughs. "Okay, Sherlock, settle down. We're almost there." We walk along a sidewalk, overfull with people, and have to stop twice for a toddler who drops her stuffed giraffe. When there's a break ahead of us, Cooper pulls us through the gap. Though when we round a corner, I'm the one stopped in the middle of the sidewalk, slowing traffic as I stare.

"What is this place?" I ask. I look at the boardwalk stretched out in front of me and the Ferris wheel slowly spinning against the sky.

"Coney Island," Cooper says, pulling me forward. "I know it's sort of cheesy, but I've never been here and I thought you might like it."

"It's perfect," I say, putting my hand on his arm. And it is. I've been heartsick for the water ever since we left Maine. "Can we ride that first?" I ask, pointing to the Ferris wheel.

Cooper laughs. "Don't you want your name on rice first?" he asks, gesturing toward a booth off to one side. I shake my head. "Tattoo?" he asks, teasing me. Another shake. "Cotton candy?" he asks.

This time I nod. "But only the pink kind. The blue and purple freak me out." Cooper raises his eyebrow at me. "All that dye." I fake a shudder.

"Yeah, I'm sure the neon pink is all-natural," Cooper says, shaking his head at me.

We walk over to the booth selling cotton candy and he buys a large. Pink. He laughs when he sees my eyes.

"That's like a lifetime supply of cotton candy," I say. Cooper won't take any of the money I try to give him.

"This is *my* surprise," he says.

"It's a good one," I say.

"Come on," he says, pulling my hand and leading me toward the rides. I pause, breathing in the briny smell of the ocean and the sweet smell my cotton candy is giving off. I feel the warm sunshine on my face and the breeze coming off the water. Warm and cool at once.

"What are you doing?" Cooper asks.

"I want to remember this moment," I say.

"Come on," he says. "The line for the Ferris wheel isn't going to get any shorter."

"At least we have provisions," I say, holding up the enormous bag of cotton candy.

"Well, *provision*," Cooper says. "Seeing as all we have is that one thing." We walk over to the line and join behind a very large, very hairy man wearing a *Kiss Me, I'm Sexy* shirt.

Cooper cuts his eyes at me, and I have to look away to keep from laughing out loud. "Sure you don't want your name on rice?" he asks, pointing to another one of the carts parked alongside the line.

"You seem obsessed with it," I say. I pull a tuft of cotton candy off the mound and put it in my mouth.

"Well, it is a modern miracle," he says.

"The polio vaccine was a modern miracle," I respond.

"But, it's your *name written on rice*," he says.

"Fine," I say. "Hold this." I hand him the cotton candy and walk over to the vendor. "I'd like my name on rice," I say. Then I think of something better. "Well, I'd like two names on rice."

"You'll have to buy two grains of rice," he says. He makes me write the names for him on a piece of paper, then he gets to work. I get to look at them under a high-powered lens.

"Cool," I say, much less impressed with the "modern miracle" than Cooper.

I pay him five dollars, which seems like a pretty steep price for two grains of rice. He starts to put my purchases into a glass vial, but I hold out my hand. After he drops the two pieces of rice into my palm, I pull the locket free from my shirt and open it. I carefully transfer the two grains from my hand to the locket and snap it closed.

The line has barely moved when I walk back over to Cooper. He's made a serious dent in the cotton candy.

"Did you get it?" he asks.

"Yep," I say. I carefully open the locket. He peers inside.

"Two?" he asks.

"One just didn't seem like enough," I say. "I mean, how many chances in your life do you have to get your name on rice?" He nods, but keeps looking at me. I know he wants to know what's on them, but I don't say. He opens his mouth like he wants to ask, but then *Kiss Me, I'm Sexy* leaves, taking his whole family with him, and we get to move forward in line.

"Want your photo taken with the lady?" a guy asks, walking up to us. "Five dollars." Cooper shakes his head, and the guy moves down the line.

"Do you have your camera?" Cooper asks. I nod and pull it out. He puts his hand out for it, but I pull it back. "I just want to take a picture of that guy," Cooper says, pointing to a man with tattoos on every bit of visible skin.

I hand the camera over and take another bite of cotton candy while Cooper gets his photo. I laugh as a seagull tries to fly away with a whole corndog clutched in its beak. Cooper takes a couple more pictures and turns off my camera before handing it back to me.

"We're almost up," he says.

I look forward to where the Ferris wheel workers are slowly helping people off the swinging seats and guiding new people into position. When it's our turn, they warn us not to rock, and click the safety bar into place. The wheel immediately turns and sends us backward and up. It takes several stops and starts before we make it to the top.

"Amazing," I say as our seat makes the final journey to the top of the wheel. We stop there, our seat swaying gently. Spread out in front of us is a wide strip of blue water reaching to the left and right. Then above that, all of Lower Manhattan sits with its buildings sprouting out of the earth like giant porcupine quills. Barges carrying huge metal lockers trundle through the *Cerulean Haze* water.

"Thank you," I say, turning to Cooper.

He smiles at me and says, "Thank *you*." And his voice suggests that he's thanking me for more than cotton candy and your name on rice and a ride on a Ferris wheel. He takes my hand, and we sit there just swaying above everything until the wheel starts turning again and we are slowly lowered to the ground.

I'm not stupid. Okay, maybe a little. But I am smart enough to know that this is the best day of my life so far. I'm guessing it will keep at least a top ten slot for my whole life. After the Ferris wheel, we play some of the midway games, and Cooper wins a stuffed whale shark and I win a hat with a propeller on it. We spend all afternoon walking up and down the boardwalk, and end up sitting in the sand, tired and sunburned. I call Veronica so she won't worry that I'm late. She tells me to say hi to Cooper for her, which makes me blush and Cooper laugh.

"Your grandmother loves me," Cooper says. I nod and roll my eyes.

"Don't you have to walk dogs today?" I ask, trying to change the subject.

"Fig and Sebastian are doing it for me."

"You had this all planned out, didn't you?"

Cooper nods. "Even that," he says, pointing to the sky that is slowly turning pink and orange in the fading light.

"Talk about delusions of grandeur," I say. Cooper laughs and slides closer to me on the sand. He puts his arm behind me and leans back slightly, looking at the sky.

"I have a serious question for you," Cooper says.

I swallow hard. "Shoot," I respond in what I hope is a casual way.

"How would you feel about being kissed?" Cooper asks.

"Are you taking a poll?" I ask.

"It's a research project I'm working on," Cooper says. "So, theoretically, if someone wanted to kiss you, how would you feel?"

"Someone?" I ask. "Like him?" I nod toward a guy in a dirty mustard-colored hoodie walking past who keeps repeating the word *banana* over and over. The truth is, I'm stalling. I've never kissed a guy.

"Well," Cooper says. "What about me?"

"Theoretically or actually?" I ask.

"Actually." He turns to look at me. Until now, we've both been staring out over the water.

"I'd feel okay about that," I say.

"Okay?" Cooper asks, leaning toward me. I start to say *more than okay*, but then his mouth is on mine and any thought that would require words is gone.

At first, I'm nervous that I'm not doing it right, but then I just let myself float. His mouth tastes sweet like cotton candy and salty from the ocean. I had thought of kissing him before, but I always worried that he'd be too self-conscious about his mouth or that maybe he didn't like me *that way*.

I feel Cooper's fingers in my hair. Then he slides his hand forward to my cheek. His thumb bumps against my scar and, without thinking, I pull back.

"Sorry," he says quickly.

I'm the one who should say I'm sorry. Not him. But that one touch was like a switch being thrown, and now all I can think about is Rachel. How she'll never get to ride a Ferris wheel or eat cotton candy or win a propeller hat at the shooting arcade. She'll never sit on the sand with the sun on her face. She'll never be kissed ever again.

"Tell me," Cooper says.

Part of me wants to. No more hiding or pretending or lying. I look over at Cooper, at his trusting eyes. I shake my head. "I can't."

"You could," he says. "It would be okay." I shake my head again.

Cooper frowns and leans back again, looking out over the water. We sit for several minutes in silence. Finally, Cooper pushes to his feet. He reaches his hand down and pulls me up. I stand, clutching the stuffed whale shark and the hat.

He looks at his watch. "We should probably head back."

I nod, knowing something fragile just shattered between us.

"You wouldn't understand," I say, trying to fix it.

"Maybe I would," Cooper says. He touches his mouth with his hand.

"No," I say with more force than I intend. I take a deep breath, trying to make sense of the swirling thoughts in my head. "What if one day your whole life changed? You woke up that morning and things were normal, so normal that if someone asked you about it, you wouldn't even be able to tell them what you had for breakfast or what you wore or even what you did that day. But, what if later, something happened? Something terrible and irreversible? And what if that something was your fault? And suddenly everything was different. Where you lived. Who you loved. Even what you looked like."

I step out of reach, putting distance between us. "You could never understand that," I say. I start walking away. From my words. From the ache in my heart. From the look in Cooper's eyes.

We ride back to the city in silence. Sitting together, but not touching. Not looking at each other. Cooper walks with me to Veronica's apartment. I try to hand him the whale shark, but he just shakes his head. I turn to walk inside, but his voice stops me.

"I hope someday, you let someone in," he says. "Maybe he'll surprise you." He turns and walks away down the sidewalk.

I watch him until he rounds the corner, hoping he'll look back, but he doesn't. Not once.

Chapter Sixteen

The dream is different tonight. It's still Rachel in the passenger seat, but Cooper is in the car too. I keep trying to tell him to get out, that he doesn't want to be there. That he doesn't understand what's going to happen. But I can't. Then there's the accident. Followed by the screaming. Then the ambulance. But this time, instead of one stretcher, they need two. Because Rachel isn't the only one not moving. I watch as they lift Cooper into the ambulance, first folding the stretcher legs, then sliding him in. But the sheet slips and I can see his face. He's staring at me, through me. His eyes are flat and dark.

Veronica sits with me until I stop crying. I lie down and pull the blanket up over my shoulder. She stays until she thinks I'm asleep, then she goes back to her room, leaving the doors open between us. I push back under the covers and try to find sleep.

I'd been home from the hospital for only a few days when the state police emailed my father a copy of their report. Normally they don't do that, but since my dad works for the state's search and rescue, and because both of his daughters were involved, they made an exception. My dad wasn't home when it arrived. I sat in the chair in front of the desk, half of my face still a spiderweb of stitches and bandages, and read. The report said *vehicular manslaughter*, which is just a nice way of saying death by automobile. They ruled it a no-fault accident, but the report stated that the breathalyzer test they gave me came up positive. Not enough to be declared drunk, but enough. The report said they tested Rachel too, but because she was in intensive care and because she wasn't the one driving, they hadn't tested her until late morning the next day. The test was inconclusive.

The police asked me why I was driving when I didn't even have a license. But I couldn't tell them anything at all, because I couldn't remember anything about that night. The psychiatrist said that was normal, but I felt anything but. It's not normal to have a chunk of your life gone, where on one side it's your birthday and you're going to a party and on the other you're in the hospital bed and your face is half gone and your mother is crying and your father is telling you your sister is dead.

Fig is grinning when I drag myself to the diner and into the kitchen. She pulls me into the cooler and shuts the door behind us.

"My mom called Frank last night." She pauses. "He's not coming."

"How did that happen?" I ask.

"The Brunellis staged an intervention," she says. "Of course, I'm not exactly sure how it was different from family dinner night, except there was a little more yelling."

I half smile. I can't imagine being at the center of an intervention with that family. Truth be told, Grace alone could scare me into compliance.

"Grace told my mom to stop being so stupid. Joey told her if Frank came around, he'd kill him. Nonna just looked at her."

I shudder, remembering how mad Nonna was when she was making cinnamon rolls. I change my mind. Nonna is definitely scarier than Grace.

"Then they all stood around while she called him. They put him on speaker phone."

"Whoa," I say, cringing.

"It was awesome," Fig says.

"I'm sure it was," I say, thinking Fig is exactly right with her choice of words. *Awesome* is the perfect word to describe the Brunelli family. They are a force of nature— powerful and sort of frightening and definitely awesome.

"Now you," she says.

"Me what?"

Fig rolls her eyes. "You. Cooper. Beach. Sunshine. Romance?" She sees me blush. "Did he kiss you?" she asks. I nod. "I knew it," she said, grinning.

She looks at me. I'm not smiling.

"I blew it," I say. I start to tell her about the weirdness after. About how I just shut down. But Grace yells at us to get out of the refrigerator. Even though the door is probably three inches of steel and air tight, we can hear her as if she's standing right beside us.

When we emerge, Nonna's list is longer than usual. "I'm sorry," she says as she adds several things to the bottom of an already overwhelming amount of work. "We're just swamped." She gives both Fig and me a floury squeeze and hums as she walks back to her office. I smile at Fig. The real Nonna is definitely back.

Fig and I divvy up the tasks. I take everything in the kitchen and give Fig everything out front. She looks at me for a long moment, but doesn't say anything. I know she'll be back to pestering me about where I go every afternoon and when we are going to *have that talk* once things slow down, but for now I just get the narrowed eyes as she backs through the door to the front.

I am literally elbow-deep in homemade pimento cheese when my phone rings.

"I'll get it," Grace says, slipping my phone out of my pocket. All I can do is watch as she pokes the screen on my phone and says hello. "Mia can't come to the phone right now. Can I take a message?"

I close my eyes and say a prayer. *Please don't be Cooper.* Then I reverse it. *Please be Cooper.*

Grace looks at me funny while she listens to whoever is talking on the other end. "I'm confused," Grace finally says. "You're calling on *behalf* of her mother? Is her mother okay?"

She listens, then nods at me. Mom's okay. Grace focuses on my face and shrugs her shoulders as she keeps listening. "I'll tell her," she says after a bit. She listens again. "You too." I hear the beep of the call disconnecting. Grace keeps staring at the phone, but she doesn't say anything.

"What did she want?" I ask, wiping my hands on a clean towel.

"That was a nun at Our Lady of Immaculate Conception," she begins. I nod. I guessed that much. "She asked me to tell you that your mother wanted to wish you a happy birthday."

I feel my stomach drop. I'd lost track of the date in my busyness. And I wonder if my mother had them call almost a week early because my actual birthday will be forever linked with Rachel's death.

"Thanks," I say, hoping Grace will just let it drop, but this is Grace.

"What the heck is that all about, Mia?" She stands there waiting for an answer, but I don't know where to begin or if I even want to begin.

"My mother is a nun," I say, like it's the most natural statement in the whole world, which it so clearly isn't.

"How is your mother a nun? Doesn't the whole married-and-child thing kind of go against the whole nun thing?"

I take a deep breath. "She applied under special circumstances," I turn back to the mixing bowl, but Grace doesn't let up.

"What does that mean? *Special circumstances*?"

I keep mixing the cheese, willing Grace to go away, but she's not budging. I take a deep breath, keeping my chin ducked. "She had to get her marriage annulled and give up her parental rights," I say quietly, so maybe only the pimento cheese can hear. I peek at Grace. She seems completely at a loss for words. For a moment.

"What kind of mother does that?" Grace asks.

"You don't understand," I say, slightly louder.

"Mia, look at me."

A lot of people are saying that to me recently. I look up at her.

Grace's expression is fierce. "No mother should ever abandon her child."

"You don't understand," I repeat. "She had to."

"*She had to,*" she says, parroting me. "Are you actually listening to yourself?"

"I deserved it," I say, because I truly deserve every bad thing that gets thrown my way and more.

"You deserved it!" Grace is so loud that several other Brunellis come in to see what all the commotion is about. One of them is Fig. "Mia, my brother Joey there is a bum."

"Hey!" Joey says, but Grace gives him a look and he shrugs. "She's right."

"My son Danny is currently attempting to break the

world record for being fired from the most jobs. My daughter, Myra, only calls home when she needs money. I won't even go into all my other kids. Whatever you did or think you did is not reason enough for your mother to take off." The whole kitchen is quiet. "Or your father, for that matter. Family is family." Everyone in the kitchen nods, like this is some great wisdom.

I look over at Nonna, who is standing in her office doorway. I wonder how much she's told everyone.

I untie my apron and lift it over my head. "You don't understand," I say for the third time. I pick up my bag from under the counter and walk toward the back door, depositing my apron in the hamper on the way out.

"Where are you going?" Grace yells at the back of my head.

"Let her go," Nonna says as I start to walk out. "But not alone. Fig, go with her."

I open my mouth to protest, but Fig is already at my side, her backpack slung over her shoulder.

"Let's go," Fig says. She heads out the back way and I follow, leaving a kitchen full of Brunellis staring at my back, quieter than I've ever heard them.

We walk down the alley and out onto the sidewalk in silence. I stand there, not sure where to go. That's the thing with running away. It works better if you actually have a destination in mind.

Fig doesn't look at me, but at the sky. "What you need is soup," she says. She puts her hand on my arm. "Come on."

She leads me across several blocks, not saying anything, like she knows I just need quiet for a bit. Even if quiet in the city is anything but. Garbage trucks slam cans against the sidewalk. A car alarm blares in the distance. A man sings Sinatra loudly and off-key. Fig turns down an alley and suddenly we're in Chinatown. We walk another block, and then Fig ducks into a restaurant with Chinese characters on the sign and a single word in English: *Food.*

We stand in the doorway, letting our eyes adjust to the sudden darkness of the restaurant. A fountain burbles in the center of the room, surrounded by fat ceramic cats balancing vases of bamboo on their heads. A woman walks out of the back and straight toward us. She is talking to Fig in what I guess is Chinese and Fig is nodding. The woman indicates that we should pick a table. We choose a booth toward the back and slide in. I face the front door. Fig faces the kitchen. The woman talks to Fig, who keeps nodding.

"This is Mia," Fig says, pointing at me. The woman smiles and her face lights up.

"Hi," I say. This makes her smile again. She tries to hand us menus, but Fig shakes her head.

"Two dumpling soups," Fig says. The woman says something else and disappears into the kitchen.

"You speak Chinese?" I ask.

"No," Fig says, like I just asked her if she's ever walked on the moon. "But Sebastian does. And no matter how many times he tells her, she still speaks to me like I can understand."

I don't have time to consider her answer before our soup arrives, carried by none other than Sebastian. He puts the bowls down in front of us and bumps Fig to slide over so he can sit down.

"You work here?" I ask. As soon as the words are out of my mouth, I'm thinking, *Well, duh, Mia,* but Sebastian just nods. I think about his art and his job at the MoMA. It's a wonder he and Fig ever find time to spend together.

"It pays the bills," he says. Fig just rolls her eyes, making him elbow her again. Her spoon sloshes a little.

"Careful," she says. "It's hot."

I take a spoonful of my soup. "It's good."

"Just don't ask what they put in it," Sebastian says. "They won't tell you. They actually have the recipe locked in a safe in the back."

"I brought Mia here to *talk,*" Fig says. The word sounds slightly ominous. Sebastian nods and leans his head back on the seat.

"I'll go first," Sebastian says, surprising me. "Did Fig tell you how we met?"

"Sort of," I say.

"I didn't give her any details," Fig says.

"Well, we were in this group. I guess it was what you'd call a support group, but it wasn't all Oprah-y. We didn't journal and walk around affirming each other or any of that crap." I half smile. "Everyone in there . . ." He pauses. "What I mean is, to get into the group, you had to be *a victim of familial violence.*" He says it in a stilted way, like he's reading it. "Basically, someone in each one of our families hurt us." I look at him for a long moment, thinking about what he just said.

"I'm sorry," I respond, because I don't know what else to say.

"It sucks, but there it is." He shrugs. "With me, it was my mom." He looks past me. "It wasn't her fault." Fig puts a hand on his arm. "I mean, it was, but it wasn't. She was mentally ill. She used to hear voices. Thought they were angels. They told her to do things." He pauses then holds out his hands toward me. He pulls up the sleeves of his shirt, revealing the ugly scars on his arms. "I've got the same ones on my feet," he says.

Fig is biting her lip, looking like she's trying not to cry. Sebastian looks over. He hands her a napkin, but she bats it away.

"It's awful," she says, softly. Sebastian pulls his sleeves back down and sits back.

"So, there you go," Sebastian says. He points at my soup. "Eat."

I shake my head, then close my eyes, gathering courage. When we were little, Rachel and I used to dare each other to jump off the dock into the freezing cold water of the lake. If you thought about it too much, you just couldn't. You had to jump, so that by the time your brain figured out what you were doing, you were already in the water.

I'm going to tell them. It's now or never.

"My sister is dead," I say, "and it's my fault."

I can't look at either of them, just at the dumplings bobbing around in the steaming broth. Fig slides her hand across the table with her palm up. I lift my hand and put it in hers.

"So, I can't join your group because I'm the bad guy. I'm not the victim."

Fig squeezes my hand. "You're not the bad guy." she says. "Do you want to talk about it?" I start to shake my head, but then I realize that I do, if only just to say it out loud.

"It was a car accident," I say. "I was driving." She squeezes my hand. "It was late. And foggy." I leave out the bit about the drinking. I can't even remember it. I close my eyes, willing the memories to come back to me. I feel the tears sliding down my cheeks. "There was a deer—"

I start to say more, but I can't. It's like all the air got sucked out of the room, making it hard to breathe. I don't say anything else. I simply keep my eyes closed.

"That picture on your camera," Fig says. I think about when she accidentally saw the photo I took of Rachel when I first got my camera. The night she died. I look up at Fig. Tears are still rolling down her cheeks. I notice that Sebastian's eyes are wet too. "That photo . . ."

"Rachel," I say. "Her name was Rachel."

"Is that how your face got hurt?" Sebastian asks. Fig cuts her eyes at him, but I nod. No one says anything.

It's Sebastian who finally breaks the silence. "You gonna eat that?" he asks, nodding toward my soup. I shake my head and slide it across the table. Fig smiles a little and picks up her spoon. Sebastian tries to dip into her bowl, but she deflects his spoon with her own.

The waitress is back. She starts smiling at us again. "It was good?" she asks.

I nod, trying to keep my face hidden behind my hair. Fig nods, and Sebastian nods with his mouth full. She takes the empty bowl from Sebastian and Fig slides hers over to take its place, shaking her head at him. The Chinese woman walks away and returns with fortune cookies clutched in her hand. She puts them down in the center of the table and walks away again. Fig nods at me, and I take one. She selects one and pushes the other toward Sebastian. We all open them. Fig and me with our hands, Sebastian with his teeth.

Fig clears her throat. "New friends are like silver. Old ones like gold." She tosses the fortune on the table and snorts. "That's so not true."

Sebastian pulls his fortune free. "A beautiful woman will buy you ice cream."

"It does not say that," Fig says, snatching the fortune from him. "He who knows he has enough is rich."

"Have you noticed they're never fortunes anymore, just pithy sayings?" Sebastian asks.

"Pithy?" Fig asks.

"You know, clever, wise."

"I know what it means," she says. "I'm just surprised to hear you use that word."

"I'm smart," he says.

"You are," Fig says. She leans against him and looks at me. "What does yours say?"

I look at the slip of paper in my hand and turn it over. "Nothing," I say. "Mine's blank."

Fig holds out her hand and I give her the slip of paper. "Weird," she says, turning it over. "I've had cookies without a fortune in them, but I've never seen a blank one."

"No pithy saying for you," Sebastian says, smiling.

"Yeah," I reply, trying to smile back.

"So," Sebastian says, leaning toward me. "Tell us what Cooper is up to."

"It's supposed to be a secret," Fig reminds him.

"But Mia knows," he says.

"Mia is in the circle of trust."

I frown. I'm not so sure about that anymore.

"Oh, and we're not?" he asks.

Fig rolls her eyes. "We are. But you can still have surprises in the circle of trust."

"What kind of name is There?" Sebastian asks. I shrug.

"It's the same guy who owns Here," Fig says.

"You mean that breakfast place uptown?" Sebastian asks. Fig nods.

The waitress is back and talking faster than before. Sebastian stands up. "Gotta get back to work." He starts to walk toward the kitchen but stops halfway. "Did you get something to wear for the opening at the MoMA?" Sebastian asks. Fig shakes her head, making him frown.

"I will," she says. She pretends to cross her heart, making Sebastian roll his eyes.

"It's in less than a week," he says, clearly stressed that she still hasn't made her fashion arrangements. He shakes his head at Fig's smile and heads toward the kitchen. "Make Mia come," Sebastian calls over his shoulder.

"You *should* come," Fig says to me.

"To what?" I ask, still feeling sort of fuzzy after the intense conversation. Obviously, Fig and Sebastian are used to this sort of thing.

"There's this event over at the MoMA. Very fancy. Some donors' party. All the volunteers get to go though and they can bring a guest." She shrugs. "Or two."

"Or two?"

"It's fine," she says. "Last winter, Sebastian brought me and Sarah *and* Cooper." The mention of his name sends a jolt through my heart.

"I don't have anything to wear to something fancy," I say, thinking about my ugly skirt and the too-tight shoes my grandmother loaned to me.

"Mia? This is New York. I'm pretty sure we can find you something to wear."

"I don't know," I say.

"Cooper will be there." I shake my head. I know she thinks that will sell me on going, but it has the opposite effect.

"Just come," she says. She looks at me for a long moment. "For me."

I sigh. "Okay," I say. "I'll go."

"Yay," she says. "I'm going to call my cousin, Rina. She's the shopping queen. She'll find us the best dresses in all of Manhattan."

She pulls out her cell and dials the Shopping Queen. While she talks, I pick up my fortune and turn it over in my hand. Still blank. When we stand up to go, Fig takes it out of my hand and leaves it on the table.

"You don't need this," she says. "Come on. Let's go shopping." The owner of the restaurant yells something at us as we walk out. "You too!" Fig calls.

"You too what?" I ask. Fig just shrugs and starts laughing. That makes me smile. She nudges me.

"Ready?" Fig asks.

"Ready." And part of me does feel ready, at least more than I did a couple of hours ago. Because while I didn't tell them everything, just telling them something made it a tiny bit easier.

Chapter Seventeen

There are two great things about Rina. First, she says she knows exactly where we can find *appropriate semi-formal wear.* That's the name she gives the kind of dresses we need after Fig describes the MoMA event. Second, her presence makes it impossible for Fig to question me further about the trip to Coney Island. Though part of me wants to tell her, especially now that I've told her a bit about Rachel.

"When is this event again?" Rina asks.

"This weekend," Fig says.

"I'm glad you didn't wait until the last minute to find something to wear," Rina says. She flips her hair away from her face, which she does a lot.

"Me too," Fig says. Either she misses the sarcasm in her cousin's voice or chooses to ignore it. "Last year I just grabbed something out of my closet, but this year I want something . . ."

"Fabulous," Rina says. Fig nods. Rina turns toward me. "I know what Fig likes, but what about you?" She pulls her sunglasses down to peer over them, and I notice her eyes are the color of the lake at twilight.

"I don't know," I say. I'm thinking she doesn't want to know that I like pie and red dogs and artistic guys. Rina looks at my face for a long moment, then she gives all of me the once-over. I'm certain I look less than *fabulous* at the moment, with jeans still dusted with flour and even the good side of my face red and puffy from crying.

"She's an artist," Fig says, nodding toward me.

Rina furrows her brow, thinking, and then she looks up at us. "I've got the perfect place."

She leads us across several blocks, leaving Chinatown behind and threading our way through to what Fig tells me is Nolita (North of Little Italy). Buildings bristle with signs advertising yoga classes and art lessons. We have to hurry to keep up with Rina. Even in her three-inch heels— which she's already told us are Manolo Blahniks she got for a steal—she is nearly half a block ahead of us by the time she turns and heads up a flight of stairs. We draw even with the shop she is entering. *Exit Stage Right* is printed in curly gold script on the window. We climb the stairs and push open the door. The inside of the shop is packed— floor-to-ceiling packed—with just about anything you can imagine. A huge orange lounge chair takes up the space in front of the counter. It's draped with feather boas and belts and mounded with boots and high-heeled shoes and ice skates. While Rina talks to a woman near the back of the store, we wait, looking around at the hills of random objects surrounding us.

Rina walks toward us with the tiny woman in tow. Seriously tiny. She's wearing high-heeled boots and yet she still barely clears Fig's shoulder.

"Madame Alexander, this is Fig and Mia," she says, gesturing toward first Fig, then me. "Ladies, this is Madame Alexander. She owns this shop."

"Call me Mimi," the tiny woman says in a thick accent, which makes me think of *Doctor Zhivago*.

"Mimi buys old props from plays and movies and then resells them here," Rina says.

"Cool," Fig says. I nod; it is pretty cool.

Mimi leads us through the store, giving a tour of many of the objects hanging from the walls and draped over pieces of furniture. She stops at a rack and pulls from it a bright blue dress that is the exact shade of Fig's hair. But when she holds it up to Fig, she quickly shakes her head.

"Too much blue," she says. She rifles through the dresses hung on the rack and pulls out another, this one a soft silvery color. "Go try this on," she says, passing it to Fig.

Rina leads the way to the back of the store, leaving me alone with Mimi. She studies me for several moments. I duck my head under her scrutiny, but she touches my chin and lifts my face.

She smiles at me and nods. "Maybe," she mutters to herself.

She gestures for me to follow her, but instead of leading me to the dressing room where I can hear Fig laughing, she takes me farther, into what looks like the stock room. After she turns on a light, which illuminates racks and racks of hanging storage bags, Mimi walks straight to the back and then to the right. I wait in the doorway, afraid to touch anything until Mimi returns bearing one of the bags.

She holds it up, but I can't see inside. She looks from me to the bag and back again several times. "Perfect," she says. "Come."

We walk back out into the store and toward the dressing rooms. Fig is standing in front of a three-way mirror and smiling at herself.

"Wow," I say. Fig's dress is strapless and falls to the middle of her calf. The best color I can think to call it is pewter. Or *Silver Bells* or *Sterling Dreams*. The satin seems to glow like the evening sky. The fitted waist flares into a huge skirt with several layers of fabric underneath, which makes it stand away from her legs. Fig is smiling at me.

"It is sort of wow, isn't it?" Rina and I both nod. Fig spins in a circle, making the skirt float upward a little.

"That's from an off-Broadway performance of *Grease*," Mimi says.

"Seriously? Amazing." Fig twirls again, which makes Mimi smile. "What about you?" she asks me.

I shrug; I still haven't seen what Mimi is holding.

"Come," Mimi says, leading me toward the other dressing room. She hangs the bag up inside the room and unzips it, then lifts out two hangers.

"Put this one on first," she says, holding up a silky green sheath. "And this one on top of it." She holds up a purple dress made of velvet.

She leaves me alone in the room, pulling the door shut behind her. I kick off my sneakers and slip out of my jeans and T-shirt. I pull the green dress on first, then slip the purple dress over it as Mimi instructed. The green sheath floats almost to my ankles, but even with the two layers, it feels light and soft. The purple dress is cut close near my neck at the front, but has a deep V at the back, making me grateful for the green silk peeking out. I tuck my locket under the collar so it won't show.

"Come out!" Fig says. There isn't a mirror inside the dressing room, so I have no choice but to walk out to the three-way mirror Fig was using. I make my way out, careful to keep my steps short to accommodate the narrow dress. I walk toward where Rina, Fig, and Mimi are standing, looking at me. None of them says anything. I duck my head slightly. I'm not sure who I was fooling. I can barely pull off normal. Forget fabulous.

"I don't know what to say," Rina says.

"What's more than wow?" Fig asks.

Mimi takes my arm and turns me toward the mirrors. "Look, honey."

I peek up at the mirror straight in front of me. I'm

careful to keep my gaze on the dress, not on my face. Now I don't know what to say.

"It's from *The Great Gatsby*," Mimi says. "One of my personal favorites."

"You look amazing," Fig says, stepping up behind me. Rina just bobs her head. Fig turns to Mimi. "We'll take them," she says.

"Wait," I say. "I don't really have very much I can spend."

When Fig said *shopping*, I was thinking some second-hand store where I might be able to find a passable dress. I'm pretty sure I can't afford anything in this store, much less one of Mimi's personal favorites.

Mimi puts up her hand. "They are a gift." All three of us protest, but Mimi won't hear any of it. "Rina will bring another one of her clients in here and they will buy thousands of dollars of beautiful things. This is the least I can do."

She leads us around the store, putting the finishing touches on our outfits. Fig gets a set of silver satin heels that match her dress and a black silk wrap covered with ornate embroidery. Mimi hands me a pair of black shoes with bows on the backs and long strands of faux pearls that I have to loop around my neck several times to keep from tripping on them. We change back into our regular clothes and bring everything to the front where Mimi is waiting.

Mimi zips the dresses back into hanging bags and wraps the other items in paper before tucking them into brown shopping bags. The whole time she works, she gives us explicit instructions on how to care for everything. The bells on the door jingle as we are saying goodbye. Mimi hugs each of us, making us promise to bring by pictures of our party. Fig assures her that I'm an excellent photographer and that I'll be documenting the whole evening.

Mimi presses something into Rina's hand and shoos us out the door. We walk down to the sidewalk, where we pause, shifting our various bags so that we can carry them more easily.

"Look at this," Rina says. We look at her outstretched hand.

"It's a locket," Fig says.

"A pretty one," Rina says, sliding the chain over her head so that the locket rests against her chest. "I'll have to figure out what to put in it."

"You're supposed to put something inside that brings you joy," I say, repeating what Rachel told me.

"What's inside yours?" Fig asks, nodding at my necklace, which has come free from my shirt. I pause, unsure of what to say. I don't really want to explain the grains of rice in front of Rina.

"It's probably personal, nosy pants," Rina tells Fig. Fig apologizes, but keeps looking at me. Rina pays for a cab so we don't have to walk across half of lower Manhattan with our arms full of packages. They drop me off at my grandmother's building, and Fig follows me out onto the sidewalk when the cab stops.

"You okay?" she asks. I nod. She narrows her eyes at

me. "You call me if you aren't," she says. I nod again. "Do it, or I swear I'll tell Nonna to invite you to family dinner night."

This makes me smile. "I promise," I say.

The cab driver honks, and Fig climbs back into the cab and shuts the door. She makes a face at me and waves as the cab pulls away. I stand there, my arms full of packages, watching them go.

I check my phone while I'm waiting for the elevator, hoping for something from Cooper, but there's only one text, and it's from my dad. The photo is so blurry, all I can see is his murky reflection in a window. An accidental selfie taken in a window looking out onto a big field. I shake my head and push my phone back into my pocket.

I consider the conflicting emotions all the way up in the elevator. Happy it was my dad, but disappointed it wasn't Cooper. I step off the elevator, juggling my packages to reach my keys. It isn't until I'm almost all the way to Veronica's apartment that I see her.

Sarah. She's sitting beside the apartment door, waiting for me. She stands as I walk toward her. "Can we talk?"

Chapter Eighteen

I lead Sarah into the apartment, feeling confused and not a little nervous. I hang the dress in the front closet and slide the bag with the shoes and necklaces in it on the floor below.

"Want some tea?" I ask, not sure what else to say.

"Sure," she says. She pulls her sleeves down over her fingers and I realize she's just as nervous as I am. She follows me into the kitchen, where I fill the kettle and put it on the stove. Then I pull two mugs down from the cabinet. That's when I notice my grandmother's note.

Planning meeting at the museum. I'll be home for dinner. Please set the table for three.

Sarah clears her throat. I turn and look at her. "I, umm . . ." she falters, and looks at me. There are tears in her eyes. As she closes them, the tears squeeze out from under her lashes and slide down her cheeks.

She looks at me again. "You can't break Cooper's heart," she says fiercely. I turn back toward the stove and stare at the blue flame flickering under the kettle. This is one of the last things I want to talk about.

"I'm not trying to break his heart," I say. And it's true. I don't want to hurt him. I want to protect him. From me. And maybe at the same time, protect me from him.

"What did he tell you?" Sarah asks. I look at her for a long moment. "About me?"

I shake my head. "Nothing," I say. "Not really." The truth is, he rarely mentions Sarah. I get the feeling she's off-limits.

Sarah pulls something out of her bag and hands it to me. It's an overexposed photo of two kids, a boy and a girl. The boy is tall and thin with dark brown hair that hangs into his eyes. I immediately know who it is. It's the eyes. Green and intense. Cooper. He has his arm around the girl and she's leaning against him a little and smiling. Her face is open and happy. It's Sarah, but not like the Sarah standing in front of me.

"This was taken two years ago," she says. "At Christmas." I look at her, and then back down at the photo. It's then that I realize what's wrong, or maybe what's right. It's Cooper's mouth. In the photo his face is whole, unscarred.

I look up at Sarah, confused. "I thought he was born that way. I just assumed."

Sarah nods. "You're thinking of cleft palates. People are born with that, but usually they have it fixed when they're young."

"Can't they fix Cooper's mouth?" I ask, wondering what could have caused his scars.

Sarah closes her eyes again. "He won't."

I think about how I told him he couldn't imagine what it was like to be normal one second and then have your whole face destroyed the next. I feel the shame of my words rise in me.

"What happened?" I ask. It's out of my mouth before I can stop it. "You don't have to tell me if you don't want to."

"It's okay," she says. "Cooper doesn't talk about it much. I guess it's easier for me. Sebastian told me that he and Fig told you about 'our group.'" She makes quotes with her fingers and half smiles at me. I register what she just said: *our group.*

"Word gets around fast," I say. The kettle starts whistling, making me jump. I take it away from the heat and turn off the flame.

"Can we sit down?" Sarah asks. I nod and follow her into the living room, leaving the empty mugs on the counter. I sit on the sofa, letting Sarah have the chair near the window.

"Our mom—Coop's and mine—had a lot of boyfriends. Most of them were harmless. Losers who hung around and ate our food and stole money from our piggy banks." Sarah smiles at me, but it's not genuine. "But there was this one. Phil. He told us to call him Uncle Phil. Cliché, right?"

The quick, false smile plays at the corners of her mouth again, but it's gone almost as fast as it appeared. "Phil was different. Mean. Not loud mean, but quiet mean. Scary mean." Sarah shivers even though the room is warm, and I realize my arms are covered with goose bumps too. "He used to watch me." She says this so softly that I find myself leaning forward. "I tried to stay out of his way. Tried to never be alone with him. Cooper told our mom about him, but she wouldn't listen."

Sarah stares at her hands twisting in her lap. "That Christmas. The one in the photo . . ." She gestures her head toward the picture I still have in my hands. "Our mom went down to the market to buy another bottle of wine, leaving us alone with Phil. Cooper and I remained in his room, but as soon as my mom was gone, Phil was at the door, knocking." Sarah pauses again and rubs her arms.

"You don't have to tell me," I say, but Sarah shakes her head.

"I want to. It's important you understand." She looks at me with the same intensity I see in Cooper's eyes. I bob my head in understanding and wait.

Sarah looks out the window, as if finding courage in the small bit of blue sky visible from the window. "Phil told me he needed help with the dishes. Told Cooper to stay in his room." Sarah frowns. "Cooper tried to follow, but Phil said something to him. Low, so I couldn't hear. I remember Cooper getting pale and nodding." She glances over at me, but looks away almost immediately. "Cooper didn't follow us. He just stood in the doorway." Sarah closes her eyes for a moment, and I wonder if she's seeing a memory that haunts her too.

"Phil led me into the kitchen. Told me to wash, he'd dry, like we were some regular family." Sarah shudders again. "I was at the sink. He pressed himself up against me, behind me. He started touching me. I completely froze. I didn't know what to do. But then Cooper was there, grabbing Phil's arm and pulling him away from me. Screaming at him."

I nod. I don't know Cooper that well, but I know he would protect Sarah from anything.

"But Cooper was only fourteen, and Phil was big. And strong." Sarah looks back at me, but this time she doesn't look away. "He hurt Cooper, broke his wrist. Had him on the ground and kicked his face." I feel a wave of nausea wash over me. "I started screaming, trying to pull him off Cooper, but Phil pushed me down and I fell against the sink. I hit my head." Sarah takes a deep breath. "After that I only remember things in bumps. Like a movie that's not edited right. You know?"

"I know," I say, thinking of the accident. How it's almost like a stop-action film in my head.

"I remember my mom bent over me, then over Cooper. Next, police. The neighbors must have called. After that, an ambulance. They checked me. Told my mom I was okay. But they took Cooper with them."

I remember when they took Rachel from me. I remember wondering if I'd ever see her again.

"The medics asked our mom if she wanted to ride along, but she said she wanted to stay with me. I thought she was afraid of leaving me alone with Phil." Sarah shakes her head, her mouth a thin line. "She wanted to stay and talk to the police. Phil said Cooper just went crazy, started attacking him. He even said Cooper hurt me. I was so out of it—" Sarah starts to cry.

"And you were scared," I say.

She nods, but tears are still running down her cheeks. "I don't know if the police believed them. They said they'd wanted to question Phil further after they talked to Cooper. Told him and my mom not to leave town or even leave the apartment." Sarah gets quiet. "I was so scared that I sat on Cooper's bed, waiting." She swallows hard, but then looks at me. "I could hear my mom and Phil talking, hear drawers being opened and closed, then an argument. Just their voices, not words.

"Soon, Phil came in." Sarah closes her eyes. "He said if I told the police the truth about what happened, he'd kill Cooper." She takes a shuddering breath. "I believed him. Then he left." She looks at me. "They both left."

Sarah leans her head back on the chair and looks out the window. "At first I thought they were just out. I chained the door, thinking I could *keep* them out, but as the day wore on and then it was night and then day again, I started thinking they weren't coming back. The police came to ask me more questions, but I was afraid to tell them anything. Afraid that Phil would come back. Afraid he meant what he said about killing Cooper. I kept thinking our mom would come back, but she didn't."

"And Cooper was in the hospital," I say.

Sarah nods. "They wouldn't let me see him at first, but the social worker they assigned us got them to let me visit." She closes her eyes. "It was bad. His arm was in a cast and they had to wire his jaw. But the whole time he kept asking how I was. Asking if I was okay. He kept apologizing for leaving me alone." She shakes her head. "His arm was broken, and his face was a mess of stitches, but he was more worried about the bump on my head and the bruise on my cheek. Cooper blamed himself."

I give Sarah a meaningful look. I understand blame.

She stares at me for a long moment, and like her brother, I can almost feel her looking inside of me. "I think that's why he wouldn't let them fix his mouth. I think he believes he deserves to be that way for leaving me." She takes a deep breath. "Cooper didn't let anyone in for a long time. No one. He went to group with me at first because I asked him to. But he wouldn't talk about it. Then one day he just decided to. First in group, and then with other people. He started helping them too."

I wonder if that's what he was doing with me: *helping me*. Part of me is grateful that he cared, but I don't want to be his charity or his good deed. I want to be his friend and maybe more than his friend.

"But then you arrived." Sarah smiles at me. "Mia, with you it's different. He's not only talking about things. He's starting to really feel things again." She leans forward and taps the photo in my hand. "That's what got lost two years ago. Not Cooper's lip or our mother. Them." I nod and look at the photo. Cooper's smile. His eyes and Sarah's face. So open.

"He trusts you, Mia," Sarah says.

I shake my head. "He shouldn't." I think of all the times I could have told him about me. About Rachel. About my face. About my mom and my dad and my life.

"He does," Sarah says. I look up at her. "And I do too." She smiles at me. "So, don't break his heart."

She stands and picks up her bag. I try to hand the photo back to her, but she shakes her head.

"You keep it," she says.

She starts toward the door, and I follow. She opens the door, steps out into the hall, and begins to walk down to the elevator. I follow, and wait with her while the car comes and the doors open. Sarah hugs me and steps into the elevator, but she puts her hand against the door to stop it from closing.

"I'll see you on Saturday," she says, smiling.

With a gentle click, the doors slide shut, and Sarah is gone.

Chapter Nineteen

I walk back into the apartment and shut the door firmly behind me. The air tastes stale, like it's been breathed in and out too many times. I walk to the window near Veronica's chair and open it as far as it will go. I hang my head out, feeling the breeze threading between the buildings. It smells salty and it makes me think of Coney Island and then of the beach near our house in Maine.

I pick up the album Veronica showed to Cooper and sit in the chair near the window. The first photo is of our house in Maine after a big snowstorm. A drift obscures most of the first floor. Then there's one of my mother elbow deep in soapy water, surrounded by canning jars ready for pickles. I flip more pages. My dad hauling his traps. Rachel learning to ride a two-wheeler. Me blowing out birthday candles.

There's a bulge at the back of the album. I flip forward. A bundle of envelopes. I pull them apart. All of them are addressed to Veronica in my father's sloping handwriting. Short notes fall from the envelopes.

I hope you're doing well. Hope to see you soon. —David.

Thought you'd want to see Mia's giant birthday cake. —David.

Dozens of them, always from my father. I flip the pages again and see the photo of Rachel and me. I lay the picture Sarah gave me beside it and think about what she said—about things lost. Too many things to count.

I hear the key in the lock, then the soft clink of Veronica's purse as she places it on the table in the hall and the sounds of shoes on the wood floor. I quickly stuff the envelopes into the back of the album. I feel like I've been spying, but then, it's my life in that album.

"Hi," I say as she rounds the corner. "I was just—" Veronica's eyes move from mine to the album still in my hands, then back to my face.

"I'm sorry." I hurry to replace the album in the bookcase. In my haste, the envelopes fall free, scattering across the carpet. I try to gather them back together, but my fingers are clumsy and I keep dropping them. I hear Veronica walking toward me, then feel her hand on my shoulder.

"Mia," Veronica says, touching my shoulder. "It's okay."

Her voice stills my hands. "Come on," she says. "My old bones can't take crouching on the floor like a wild animal." I glance at her, surprised to see her smiling.

She walks to the sofa and sits, nodding toward the other end of the couch. Neither of us says anything for a few moments. Veronica is looking past my shoulder, out the window behind me. I just stare at my hands, still clutching Sarah's photo.

"Thank you," my grandmother says, finally.

"For what?" I ask. It's about the last thing I would have imagined her saying.

"Before you came here, my life was neat and tidy. There were no elbows on my dinner table. No soup being slurped. No friends dropping in at the last minute for dinner." I cringe a little. "My life was orderly and predictable and—empty."

"Then I got dumped on you," I say.

Veronica frowns at me. "Mia, I *asked* your father to bring you here. He was reluctant, but I insisted that what you both needed was a little space to breathe. Plus, I wanted you here."

The information about my father is news to me. "It didn't seem like you wanted me," I say, remembering those first days.

Veronica sighs. "I'm not the best at . . ." She pauses then looks at me. "I want relationships, but I'm not that great at starting them or keeping them."

"You're better than I am," I say.

She smiles. "I've wanted to meet my granddaughters

ever since you were born." The plural *granddaughters* hangs between us.

I say what she won't. "And because of me you'll never meet Rachel,"

"Mia, look at me." I meet her eyes. "Rachel is dead, but you aren't." I open my mouth to say something, but she holds up her hand. "It's harsh, but there it is." Her face is kind but determined. "And," she says, pausing before making her second point, "Rachel wouldn't want you living as if you were."

She looks at me fiercely, as if daring me to disagree. I stare down at my hands. She's right, of course.

"I don't even know where to start," I say.

Veronica sighs. "I think you start the same place I did with your mother. You say you're sorry." I look up at her. This is the first time she's talked about what happened between her and my mom. All I have is my mother's side of things. "From the moment your mother turned five and ran halfway across Central Park, forcing me to chase her, we battled. She was a free spirit, and I was determined that she follow my plans." She shakes her head. "And I'm afraid the more I made rules, the more she broke them. And the more she broke them, the more rules I tried to enforce." She smiles at me. "And then she met your father. And you girls came along. And I guess somewhere in the middle of that, I grew up. I learned that loving someone means loving them no matter what." She sighs again. "But I guess there were just too many bad memories between us for her."

"But maybe that's it," I say. "Maybe there are too many bad memories."

"Maybe," she says. She looks at me. "All you can do is say you're sorry and then keep at it, working to make things right."

"But I can't make everything right," I say.

Veronica shakes her head. "No, you can't. I couldn't either. Your mother couldn't ever forgive me for being so horrible when they first got married, but your father could." The pain on Veronica's face is raw. "And so you do what you can. You keep moving forward, piecing things together. Some things can't ever be fixed. Some things can."

She softly grins at me. "But the best things are the ones that, when they are put back together are even stronger than before."

I think about Rachel and my mom and my dad. I think about Cooper. Everything just feels too overwhelming.

Veronica reaches out and places a hand on mine. "Just start with one thing." She checks her watch, and her eyes go big. "And I know just the thing," she says, already heading toward the kitchen. She returns, handing me a twenty. "I'll get dinner going. You go find dessert."

I grab my bag and head for the door. "Get enough for three," she says, making my heart bump.

Cooper. Please let it be Cooper.

I'm almost all the way out the door when I hear Veronica's voice. "Mia! Nothing with avocados," she calls after me, and I smile.

Chapter Twenty

The Little Bakeshop has too many cupcake flavors to decide on just three, so I buy half a dozen, including Gone Bananas, Orangearific, Moon and Stars, Walnuttiest, Chocolate Mooses, and OREO You Didn't. I'm back out on the sidewalk with my pink box of goodness, hurrying back to the apartment, barely daring to admit what I hope.

I cross the street and head to the park. Little pops of nervousness keep floating through my head as I oscillate between wanting and then not wanting to see Cooper. I step into the park and walk past two old men hunched over a chess board and a man wearing a Clash T-shirt creating giant bubbles with a bucket of bubble junk and a piece of cording.

My phone buzzes in my pocket. I pull it out and click

open the photo. It's of the bubble guy. And a thumb. I look up and see him. There on the other side of the sidewalk.

My father.

"Hi, Mia-bird," he says, walking toward me. He rubs the back of his neck and looks at me. *At me.* "Guess you're surprised to see me here," he says.

He has no idea.

I just look at him. He seems out of place. Jeans and a plaid shirt and boots. His multitool is still tucked in his shirt pocket and he has his hunting knife strapped to his boot.

"I wanted to see you," my father says.

"Really," I say, surprised at the anger in that one word. Seeing me is the last thing he's wanted to do in almost a year. He rubs the back of his neck again.

"Why are you really here?" I ask. Seeing him is like seeing part of a dream I barely remember. My father takes a step toward me, making me pull back. He pauses.

"Mia," he says. His voice catches and he closes his eyes. "I'm so sorry."

Those are the words I should be saying to my father. He's saying them to me.

"About what?" I ask. He doesn't say anything. "Because if you're sorry about losing Rachel, I already know that."

"Of course I'm sorry that Rachel is gone. I think about her every day." I lower my head and examine my feet. "But that's not why I'm here. Mia . . ."

I look up at him and find he's still looking at me. Right at me. At my face.

"It's you I'm sorry about. I'm sorry about losing *you*."
His voice is so soft, I almost can't hear him.

"What did you say?" I ask.

"I'm sorry that I lost you."

"You didn't *lose* me," I say. "You knew where I was." I
frown at the giant bubble that floats behind him. "You just
couldn't bear to look at me."

"I'm looking now," he says.

"Are you?" I ask. I turn the ruined side of my face to
him, but I don't take my eyes off him. "Are you really looking? Do you see this?" I ask.

I point to the ropey scar that almost looks like it's just
lying on my face instead of part of it. Anger boils up inside of
me, pressing against the guilt and sadness. And I don't know
whether to scream or cry or pound my fists against the ground.

My father just nods, but his eyes are wet. "I'm so sorry,"
he says again. "I hope—" His voice breaks and he's silent.

"What do you hope?" I ask. All the things I hope for are
impossible. Time machines and magical watches that let
you flip back a whole year—they don't exist. Nothing can
fix what happened.

"I hope someday you can forgive me," he says. He shoves
his hands into the pockets of his Carhartts.

"I hope someday you can forgive me too," I say, because
I know both of those things are welded together.

He reaches out and touches my cheek, and for once I
don't pull away. "Look at me," he says. I do, but just for a
moment. "There's nothing to forgive."

"I got my sister killed," I say. "I'm pretty sure that falls into the category of Things You Need to Be Forgiven For."

"It was an accident," my father says. I shake my head. Everyone says that, but I was driving. It was my fault.

"If you need me to say it, I will," he says. "I forgive you." He pauses, making me look up. "I forgive Rachel too."

"What? It wasn't her fault." All I feel when I think of Rachel is pain. Like every memory I have of her is veiled in sadness and shame.

"Rachel was drunk," Dad says. He nods when he sees the surprise in my eyes. "She shouldn't have taken you to that party. She was your big sister. She should have been looking out for you."

"You can't—" I begin.

"Yes, I can," he says. "Everyone says you can't talk bad about the dead, but no one seems to have a problem talking bad about the living." He looks at me for a long moment, letting me know that he's aware of the things people said about me after the accident.

"I don't want to live in the past anymore, Mia. Do you?" he asks.

I shake my head. I don't, but I don't know how not to.

"We'll work on that together," he says. He must see something in my eyes. "Please," he says. "We'll just take it slow."

"Slow would be good," I say, because I know if I'm going to trust him again, it's going to take a long time.

"I've missed you, Mia-bird," he says.

"Me too," I respond, because if nothing else, I know that much is true.

I look past him toward the dog park, feeling the ache of missing in my heart that stretches beyond this moment. The ache that isn't just about the past, but about the future too. It's then that I see the people walking past. See them staring at my father.

"What?" he asks, seeing the smile on my face. I shake my head and start laughing a little. I can't help it because I'm looking at his Bean boots and his flannel shirt and his woven belt that has little pockets and clips all over it. And it all feels so familiar, but it's all so out of place here. And then I'm full-out laughing, thinking about my father walking from Penn Station to my grandmother's apartment, looking like he took a wrong turn somewhere at the Vermont border and ended up here.

"I'm glad you're here, Dad," I say. And I am.

"You sure?" he asks. "I told Veronica that I wasn't sure if you wanted to see me, but she said you did."

"Are you staying?" I ask.

"For a few days," he says. "We'll talk about it, okay?"

"Okay," I say. We stand there awkwardly for a few moments, neither of us willing to make the first step toward the other. Then he hugs me. I have to be careful not to drop the pink bakery box. We stand like that in the middle of the sidewalk, making people walk around us. Then his stomach growls. He pulls away, looking sheepish.

"Sorry," he says. "I'm starving."

I smile. My father is always hungry. Always. "Let's go eat dinner," I say, pulling back from him.

We walk beside each other, keeping a safe distance. I know we both need time.

Chapter Twenty-One

Veronica acts like there's nothing out of the ordinary when we walk in together.

"Why don't the two of you get cleaned up for dinner?" she says from the doorway. I show my father where the bathroom is, then I walk back to the kitchen and wash my hands at the sink. A moment later, my father comes around the corner. His cheeks are pink and his hair is damp.

"Veronica, do you have a mop? I notice I left some footprints behind."

She looks at the size 12 muddy footprints in her hall. At first I'm afraid she's angry, but then she starts laughing, making my father's cheeks even pinker.

"Something smells amazing," Dad says. "Although I have to confess that after more than a month of nothing but rehydrated spaghetti bolognaise, I'm up for just about anything. What are we having?"

Veronica starts laughing even harder. She lifts the lid to the pot on the stove.

"Spaghetti," she says.

My father looks sheepish. "I'm sure it's better than what I've been making."

Veronica flips off the burner and puts the cover back on the pot. "Let's go out," she says. "I know this great little place." She looks over at me and I nod. Family dinner night with my family.

The word *family* trips me up for just a moment, because a year ago my family looked very different, but watching my dad and Veronica laugh together while he tries to operate a mop and she tries not to tell him he's doing it all wrong makes me smile. There aren't as many of us and we aren't as emotive at the Brunellis, but maybe with time we can be stronger than we once were.

"Let's go," I say. "I'm starving." My dad smiles at me and I smile back, because for the first time it feels like it's okay . . . or at least it's going to be.

Even though he has about eight inches on her and outweighs her by probably seventy pounds, Grace is definitely frightening my dad.

"So, you decided to come back," she says when I introduce

her. My dad nervously bobs his head yes. "Well," Grace says, frowning, "at least that's something."

Gina directs us to a booth and leaves us with menus. It's weird being a customer here. Fig waves from behind the counter, and I wave back. The rest of the family seems to be watching us while trying to pretend not to watch us.

"So, what's good here?" my father asks.

"Everything," Gina says, returning with a basket of rolls and twin dishes of honey butter and homemade jam. My father decides on minestrone soup and chicken and dumplings. I decide to have the same. Veronica hands her menu to Gina.

"Make it three," she says. We sit not talking for a while, suddenly awkward now that the drama is over and there aren't any footprints to mop up.

"How are you doing?" my father finally asks me.

"Okay," I say, not sure how to condense everything into a few sentences.

Veronica gives me one of her looks. "I would say you're a little more than *okay*." She looks at my father. "Mia is apparently the best baker's helper Nonna's ever had."

I raise my eyebrows. This is definitely news to me.

"And she's taking pictures again, although I've never seen any of them." It's her turn to raise her eyebrows at me. "And she has some nice *friends*." The emphasis on the word *friends* is not lost on my father, but he doesn't say anything.

"Hi!" Fig walks over to our table. "I'm Fig," she says, holding out her hand to shake my father's.

He seems startled by her, which makes me smile. She sits down beside my grandmother and begins talking and talking. She tells my dad about Cannoli Day and Art Attack and all the other stuff we've done over the past few weeks. My father just nods, clearly overwhelmed.

"And this Saturday, we're going to this reception at the MoMA," she tells my dad. "Mia has this amazing dress. It's all purple and green, and it has this drapey thing at the front."

My dad keeps nodding, and I can't help but laugh a little. Fashion is utterly lost on him.

"You should come," she says. "Of course, you'll have to get a suit or a tux, but probably one of my uncles could help you out."

Our food arrives, saving my father from responding. I clearly remember him saying that the only time anyone would catch him in a suit would be right before they dropped him into a six-foot-deep hole and threw dirt on him.

"Fig!" Gina calls from the kitchen.

"Gotta go," she says. She stands up. "It was super to meet you. I'm sure I'll see you again." She heads back to the kitchen, and as soon as she's out of earshot, both my father and Veronica start laughing.

"She certainly is exuberant," my father says, smiling.

"She is," I say. "She's the best."

"I'm glad you have friends here, Mia," my father says.

"Me too," I say, although right now I'm not so sure about one of them. Somehow, I have to talk to Cooper. Somehow, I have to make things right.

We're almost finished eating when Gina comes over again, bearing a plate of whoopie pies. My father takes one and bites into it.

"This is the best whoopie pie I've ever had," he announces loudly. I shake my head. Dads can be so embarrassing. He finishes one and starts on another, making me believe he really does like them. "Of course, if it were peanut butter filling . . ."

I shake my head. The forever argument at our house—peanut butter versus vanilla icing. Dad and Rachel were always for peanut butter, while my mom and I were firmly in the vanilla camp.

"Say what?" Joey says, walking over. He pulls his earbuds out of his ears. "There are different kinds?"

My dad nods and Joey glares at me. Clearly, he thinks I've been holding out on him. Joey demands to know all the other varieties of whoopie pies, and Dad and I trade off listing them until Joey's written down more than a dozen varieties. Joey shakes my father's hand like he's just been given the key to the city before heading back into the kitchen. I'm pretty sure I know what will be at the top of my list in the morning. My dad looks over at me, grinning.

"I missed you, Mia-bird," he says for the second time today.

"I missed you too, Dad," I say.

Then Joey belches long and low and Grace yells at him, and I spot Fig trying not to crack up. My dad cuts his eyes at me and I duck my head, trying not to laugh.

Chapter Twenty-Two

I tell myself I've been too busy to stop by and see Cooper, but that's not quite true. Though I have been busy. Nonna has us working harder than ever. It's wedding season, and you'd be surprised how many brides forgo a wedding cake for a huge tower of Brunelli cannolis. And after work, I've been spending time with my dad, doing the touristy stuff like taking the ferry to Staten Island and walking (yes, walking!) to the top of the Empire State Building.

But I've also been taking him to other places, like to see Sarah play at The Wall and to watch Sebastian try to beat the record for number of grapes stuffed into his mouth at once. (He managed forty-three, just twenty-eight short of the world record.) Cooper was at both places, but he stood far away from us and left without saying anything to me.

I also took my father to have dumpling soup at the restaurant where Sebastian works. My dad entertained Sebastian and Fig with stories I've heard all my life, like how he found actual buried treasure when he was doing a dive off the coast of Florida and how once he was trapped in an underwater cave for nearly an hour when his arm got wedged inside a crack in the rocks.

"I wasn't sure I was going to make it home to see my little girls again," he says. He looks at me quickly, but I just nod.

I'm getting used to talking about Rachel, or at least hearing about Rachel. I lean back and snap a photo of the side of my father's face as he talks. He doesn't even blink. I've been taking lots of photographs over the past week. All close-ups of faces. A homeless man asleep on the steps in front of our building. A woman selling beaded belts from a stand in Washington Square Park. Grace when she's yelling at Fig and me because we're goofing off instead of putting together the pans of lasagna like she asked.

"So, when am I going to meet this mystery guy you've been seeing?" my father asks, causing me to nearly drop my camera.

I shrug. "We've just been busy." Everyone looks at me. "Well, we have," I say.

Fig shakes her head. We've already had some version of this same conversation at least half a dozen times over the past few days. "Mr. Hopkins?" Fig says, looking at my dad. "How would you like me and Sebastian to take you on a tour of Chinatown?"

My father gestures "sure," and looks at me for confirmation, but Fig is already shaking her head. "Oh, Mia's not invited." She looks at me pointedly. "She has something she needs to take care of."

I roll my eyes. Fig is not exactly subtle.

My dad goes along with it. "I'll see you later," he says, and kisses the top of my head.

"You lead the way," my father says to Fig, dropping money on the table to cover our bill. He and Fig and Sebastian start toward the door, leaving me sitting at the table. Fig points at me and gives me what I suppose is her scary face before disappearing out onto the sidewalk.

The woman who owns the restaurant comes out and smiles at me. She reaches into the pocket of her apron and pulls out a fortune cookie, then places it in front of me. She smiles again as she stacks the bowls and carries them to the kitchen. I pick up the cookie and turn it over in my hand so I can I rip the plastic open. Once I've freed the cookie, I break it in two and slide out the fortune.

At least this one isn't blank. I read it, then fold it in half and start to put it in my pocket until I think better of it. I pull my locket free and push the clasp, sliding the fortune inside before snapping the locket closed and tucking it away again. I take a deep breath and walk toward the door.

The day is overcast and almost cool, and I shiver as I leave the warmth of the restaurant. I start walking farther downtown toward There, trying to figure out what I'm going to say, but even when I'm right in front of the door, I still have nothing.

The first drop of rain hits my arm. Then another and another still, until I have to either go in or start running for my grandmother's building to keep from getting totally soaked. I decide to go in, figuring I can always make a run for it later.

A lot has changed in a week. The floor is finished and a new glass case covers the whole front wall. There's a long wraparound counter with stools positioned in regular intervals along it, and tables and booths fill most of the remaining room. But it's the mural on the back wall that makes me pause. Other than the lower right-hand side where I was working on the ocean, it's complete. I walk forward, watching as it turns from one big picture into hundreds, maybe thousands of tiles, each arranged perfectly so that from afar they blend together into the perfect landscape. I reach out and touch one of the tiles that make up a maple tree with its leaves just starting to turn.

"Hey!" a voice calls from the entrance. "We're not open yet." I turn and see Simon standing there. "Sorry, Mia," he says when he realizes it's me. "Where've you been?"

I start to tell him I've been busy, you know work and family and blah, blah, blah, but one look at Simon's face tells me he's not going to accept that for a second.

"He's out back," Simon says. I take a deep breath.

"Thanks," I say, and head toward the door that leads through the kitchen and then to the alley beyond.

I've decided I'm going to tell Cooper everything—everything I can remember. I leave my bag with my camera in it on a table near the kitchen and walk outside. It's still raining, but only drizzling now. Cooper is bent over an air compressor that he has shielded from the rain with a big tarp. He's slowly pouring something white and viscous and foul smelling into a bucket connected to the compressor by a long plastic tube. He puts down the empty bucket and stands up, using his sleeve to wipe at the water that is dripping from his hair into his eyes. Then he turns toward the building and toward me.

It's in that long moment that I see the pain in his eyes that I'd always assumed was there because of his art. But then it's gone as if he's dropped a curtain over it all.

"Hey," he says finally.

"Hi," I say.

"Why are you here?" he asks, and I feel my heart bump painfully in my chest. I realize it's almost the same question I asked my father when he arrived.

"I wanted . . ." I take a deep breath, trying to remember what my father said. "I wanted to see you."

Cooper looks past me for a moment, like he's searching for the right words, but then he sighs and looks back at me. "Mia, I don't mean to be harsh, but I've really got a lot to do. Simon's trying to open next week, and I've got to finish the wall and spray it today if it's going to dry in time."

"Of course," I say. His voice is so matter of fact, and his eyes are flat. "I didn't mean to interrupt." I stare at the ground.

"It's fine," Cooper says after a long pause. I look back up at him, but I can barely stand to see him looking at me like that, Not angry, not sad. Just nothing.

"Cooper," I say. "I'm sorry."

"I'm sorry too," he says. And I desperately want him to tell me why. Is he sorry that we had an argument? That I didn't trust him? That we met? But he doesn't say any of those things. He only looks down at the bucket at his feet. "I've really got to get back to work."

"I know." I'm already backing toward the door. "I guess I'll—" I start to say, *I'll see you around*, but I know that's not very likely.

"Yeah," he says, as if he was thinking the same thing. He bends and lifts the bucket, and I walk back into the kitchen and through to the dining room and the front door.

"Did you find him?" Simon calls from the other side of the room.

"Yeah," I say, hoping that Simon will think the wetness on my cheeks is just from the rain.

"I'll see you later, Mia," Simon calls. I hear Cooper's voice as I walk out. Talking to Simon, but not to me. I step out into the rain, wondering if this is one of the things Veronica said you just can't fix.

I decide not to go straight back to Veronica's. I walk through the rain until my clothes are so wet that I'm pretty sure they wouldn't get any wetter if I jumped into the river. There's the ice cream place and the dog park. I pause under an awning, watching as a man in a suit with a newspaper clutched over his head sprints past, running for a waiting cab. The Brooklyn Bridge looms over the streets. I decide to walk on the bridge, and start to feel that ache inside of me that I thought I'd completely used up when Rachel died and then my mom left and my dad took off. But it seems my heart still has room for pain.

The walkway is mostly empty. Just me and some guy riding a bicycle away from me toward Brooklyn. It's too wet to see much of anything to either side. Just heavy gray clouds dipping into soupy gray water.

I stop at what I imagine is the halfway point and look down at the water below, which seems to stretch forever in both directions. Rain peppers the surface of the river, making it dance. The cold has brought with it fog, which is nudging up against the city, kept out by the buildings guarding the shoreline. Within minutes, the fog is so thick I can't see either side. It's just me floating on this bridge on a huge gray cloud. Even the sounds of the city, always there, are muffled. The only real noise is a foghorn calling from far away.

My parents made me see a therapist before I was released from the hospital the first time. "It's just an assessment," the doctor told me, but after the seventeenth question she asked, I knew exactly what they were trying to assess. They wanted to make sure that when they released me, I wouldn't hurt myself. She kept encouraging me to talk about everything, but no one wanted to hear how poor Mia was feeling. All anyone could think about was poor

Rachel, who died too young. She was too beautiful and too smart and too popular to die. I imagined if they thought about me at all, it was only ugly, hateful things.

I sit down and lean against one of the support posts. It's cold through my shirt. I should go back. Back to my grandmother's, or maybe all the way back to Maine. But before I can move, the fog takes over, reminding me of the way it started pressing in even as Rachel was driving us down our dirt road and out onto the highway. I close my eyes and lean my forehead against my knees, feeling rain drop onto my neck and slide under my collar. The memories are coming hard and fast now, and I let them.

Rachel told me to just relax when we pulled up in front of Greg Stinson's house. "It'll be fun," she said. She led the way up the driveway and onto the porch. The windows were vibrating with music and laughter. "You ready?" she asked, smiling at me. I nodded, but I felt anything but ready.

The kitchen was crowded with people I'd never met, some standing, some sitting on the counters, and others hunched over the keg sitting on the table. Everyone seemed to know Rachel. They smiled at me too. "Any friend of Rachel's," some guy said as he pressed a red plastic cup into my hand. I took a sip to be polite. My first beer. It was bitter, but then it settled into my stomach. Warm and heavy.

"This is Greg," Rachel said, drawing someone toward me. He nodded and grinned.

"Mia," he said. He had his hand on the back of Rachel's neck. I smiled at Greg and took another sip.

"Stinson!" someone yelled from the other side of the room. Greg glanced over and nodded his head in acknowledgment. He gave Rachel a squeeze, leaving faint white marks on the sides of her neck.

"Good to meet you, Mia," he said before walking off.

"You okay?" Rachel asked, gesturing at my cup. I told her yes because her eyes told me she needed me to be okay. Her feet were already turned toward Greg, who stood with some other guys. All laughing. Passing a bottle back and forth between them. Rachel rolled her eyes at him but was beaming.

"I'll find you in a bit," she said. When she reached Greg, he put his hand on the back of her neck again and smiled at me. I turned away from them, trying to make Rachel believe I could handle myself here. Make her believe it wasn't a mistake to bring me along.

"I'm Jack," the beer guy said. He peered into my cup. "Drink up," he said. "There's plenty where that came from." I took another sip and then another. Holding something gave me something to do with my hands. Drinking gave me something to do with my mouth.

"How do you know Rachel?" Jack asked. I followed his gaze to where Rachel was still standing with Greg, his arm now around her.

"Rachel's my sister," I said to Jack. He raised his brows, looking from me to her and back again.

"I could see that," he lied. I took another drink, a long one, feeling the warmth and heaviness in my stomach grow. "That's more like it," Jack said.

People floated past. Talking to Jack. Smiling at me. Rachel floated toward me once. Her cheeks were flushed and her eyes were big and dark.

"You okay?" she asked again. I nodded. She handed Jack two empty cups and he refilled them and handed them back. "Stick with Jack. He's nice," Rachel said.

Jack rolled his eyes. "Nice," he said. "Thanks for that." Rachel just grinned at him and walked away.

"What's wrong with nice?" I asked. My words seemed big and round, like the vowels were all misshapen from wear.

"Nice doesn't get girls like Rachel," Jack said.

"What does?" I ask.

"Greg Stinson," Jack said. "Every girl wants Greg." I watched as Rachel and Greg disappeared up the stairs.

I don't know how much time passed. Ten minutes? An hour? It was hot and close in the room. And the heaviness in my stomach was turning into something else.

"You okay?" Jack asked, looking at me. I shook my head, but the movement made my head wobble on my neck, like it wasn't attached correctly. Jack took my elbow and started steering me through the living room. He knocked on a closed door, but all he got in response was giggling. "Come on," he said. "There's another bathroom upstairs."

He piloted me toward a door and flipped on the light, pulling the door shut behind him as he left. I sat on the edge of the tub, trying to make the warm beer and the piece of lemon birthday pie be quiet. That's when I heard Rachel. I couldn't hear the words, just the tone. Part angry. Part scared. I pushed up from the tub, my heart beating too loud in my ears. I pulled open the door and followed the sound of her voice down the hall.

"Stop it," Rachel said. I stood in front of the closed door. Silence. Then, again, Rachel's voice. More panic. "Stop it, Greg."

I knocked. Nothing. "Rachel?"

"Go away." Male. Harsh. Angry.

"Rachel?" I called again. "Are you in there?"

Muffled cursing. Male. Then the door. Greg. His shirt was off and his pants were undone. He blocked the door, forcing me to look around him. "Go away," he said, glaring at me. "Your sister's busy." He smirked as he looked into the dark bedroom.

"Mia?" Rachel called.

Greg wasn't prepared for me to push my way in, and he certainly wasn't prepared for me to see. Rachel was lying sideways across the bed with her jeans bunched at her ankles. Her eyes were enormous, looking at me.

I remember helping Rachel up. Helping her find her missing clothes. Helping her stand. Helping her walk. We went past Greg, down the stairs, and out the door. Away from the music and the noise and Jack calling after us.

"Can you drive?" I asked Rachel, already knowing the answer. I pushed her into the passenger seat and buckled her in. I walked around the car and climbed behind the wheel.

Then there was Greg striding across the yard. His face red, his pride bruised, his voice loud and angry. I locked the doors. He pounded on the window. I started the car, trying to pretend I knew what I was doing. I tried to pretend I was just hauling traps from the garage to the water in my dad's old farm truck. I steered away from Greg, away from the lights and the party and the noise.

I should have called.

I should have taken the Ridge Road.

I should have seen the deer.

Everyone says to accelerate when you realize you're going to hit an animal in the road. Common knowledge where the deer outnumber the people two to one. They tell you that the force of the impact will send the animal up and over the windshield. Minimizing damage. Lessening injury. Decreasing loss. They tell you to go against your instinct to swerve or stop or even slow down.

The deer died on impact. *Didn't feel a thing,* they said.

Rachel died a short time later. *She was peaceful at the end,* they said.

I should have died. *She should have died,* they said.

They were right.

The fog keeps rolling across the bridge, cutting me off on either side. I'm alone, I think. No one can find me here. No one *will* find me here. I stand back up and stare at the water, still dancing with the rain until even that disappears. I close my eyes and wish the wish that's been right there for so long. *I wish I could disappear.* Just evaporate. Fade. Nothing dramatic. Nothing that would make the papers. Just another girl. A nobody. Gone.

But then I think about what Veronica said, about piecing things back together. And I think about what my father told my mother—that you just have to keep moving forward. And I think about Waffles sitting on my foot, trusting and sweet, and I smile.

So when I first hear a dog barking, I think I'm imaging it. But it doesn't stop, it just keeps going—deep and rhythmic. Then high and shrill. I open my eyes and stare into the fog. The barking is louder, closer. I stand and press against the railing to make space on the walkway before me. Then along with the barking, I hear the jingling of a leash and footsteps.

Samson is the first to appear. I know it's him by the crystal-studded pink collar and the ferocity in his bark. Waffles is next, pulling at his leash. Then Cooper. Samson bites at my ankles, Waffles shakes the rain from his fur, and Cooper just looks at me.

"Hey," I say, because I don't know what else to say and because I'm trying to pry Samson's mouth off the leg of my jeans. "How did you find me?" I ask.

"Well, I may or may not have been following you," he says. Cooper swipes at his forehead, brushing his wet hair out of his eyes. "I had to get the dogs, so that slowed me up, but thankfully you didn't go too far." He squints into the fog and then looks back at me. "We should talk."

"We should," I say.

"I'm sorry," he says. "I acted like a jerk."

I shrug. "So did I." I look back over the water. I remember my grandmother's advice to just start with one thing. I can hear my father's voice, telling me it wasn't my fault. I can feel Fig's hand in mine and see Sebastian's tears. I feel Sarah's arms as she hugged me and told me she trusted me. I turn and look at Cooper, aware the slight breeze is pushing my hair away from my face.

"My sister's name was Rachel. She died in a car accident. I was the one driving." And then I tell him everything. Just spill it out onto the sidewalk in front of him until I have to stop to catch my breath. When the words are gone, I close my eyes. I don't want to watch him walk away.

But then there's a bump against my leg and a heavy weight on my foot. Waffles. And a soft touch on my face. I look up at Cooper, and he brushes my cheek. I start to turn away, but his fingers find my chin.

"It's okay," he says softly. He steps closer and slides his hand behind my head. I let myself fall against him, feeling the rough fabric of his thermal shirt against my cheek. We stand like that, his arms around me and his chin on the top of my head.

"Thank you," I say. He pulls back and looks down at me. "For what?"

"For not giving up on me," I say. "For not going away." He brushes my damp hair from my cheek.

"I'm not going anywhere," he says.

He looks at me, his fingers in my hair. When his thumb brushes against my scar, I stiffen slightly, and he hesitates. But his eyes hold mine, and I feel something shift inside of me. And I nod and close my eyes, feeling his thumb on my cheek and his fingers in my hair. And for once, instead of pulling away I lean in. His touch is so gentle, I can barely feel it. He traces my scar, starting at my eyebrow and finishing where it ends just beneath my collarbone. It's the first time anyone besides a nurse or doctor have touched my scar. I look up at him, studying his face.

"What are you thinking?" I ask.

"Well," he says, "I was thinking maybe we could go somewhere drier." His voice is teasing. I make a face and start to turn away, but his fingers catch my chin. "Actually, I was just thinking how beautiful you are." I scowl at him. "Even when you make that face."

"Thank you," I say, suddenly shy.

He smiles again. "We really could talk somewhere else," he says. As if on cue, it starts raining even harder. Sheets of water pour over us.

"Somewhere else would be good," I say. Cooper hands me Waffles's leash and we head back toward the city.

"How'd you find me?" I ask.

"Well, it certainly wasn't Waffles." He nods toward his dog, who is trying to catch raindrops in his mouth. "He's sort of useless. Cute, but useless." Cooper's hand finds mine and his fingers are warm against my skin. He sees the look on my face. "Okay," he says. "like I said, I followed you. But then I didn't want it to look like I followed you, so I stopped and picked up Samson and Waffles. They're close by and I thought they made for a good cover."

"So that it would look like you were out walking the dogs and you just happened to run into me?" I ask.

"Exactly," Cooper says.

"Good plan," I say, smirking. "With your knack for subterfuge, you should be a spy."

Cooper pretends to consider my suggestion. "I'll stick with dog walking." He has to pull Samson back when the small terror goes to attack a trash bag with a dying fern hanging out of the top.

"Where to?" I ask.

"How do you feel about pie?" Cooper asks.

I raise my eyebrows. "Theoretical pie or actual pie?"

"Actual," he says.

"I feel very good about pie," I say.

"Man, I ask how you feel about kissing and you say okay. But pie gets a very good."

"You should ask me again," I say, stopping under an awning.

"Okay," he says. He stops and looks at me. "How do you feel about pie?" I shake my head and start to walk out from under the awning and into the rain. His hand on my arm stops me. "How do you feel about being kissed?" he asks. The rain keeps beating on the awning above us, loud, without rhythm.

"Okay," I say, laughing. Cooper rolls his eyes, but I pull him toward me and kiss him. "How was that?" I ask when I pull back a little.

"Definitely okay," Cooper says. This time, he kisses me.

Chapter Twenty-Three

And then what happened?" Fig asks. She bounces on the balls of her feet as we talk. I notice that the Brunelli family is unusually quiet. Listening. I make my eyes big at her and mouth the word *later.* But she just shakes her head. "They don't care," she says, gesturing at Grace, Gina, and Nonna, who are desperately trying to put the lasagna together as quietly as possible so they can eavesdrop.

"Then I kissed him," I say softly. I make my eyes big. Nonna clucks her tongue. "In my day—" she begins.

"Mother," Grace says, cutting her off. "It's totally acceptable in today's society for a girl to kiss a guy."

"Hmmpf," is Nonna's only response.

"Anyway!" Fig says over her family's critique of my love life. "And then what?"

I tell her about going to the pie shop and sitting outside so we can keep Waffles and Samson with us.

"You love pie!" Fig says, as if I need reminding.

Then I tell her how I told Cooper everything about Rachel, and my mom deciding to become a nun, and how my dad left but now he's back. By this point Gina, Grace, and Nonna are leaning against the counter and listening. Any pretense they are working is completely gone. Grace asks questions about Rachel, and Gina starts crying. And Fig rolls her eyes at Gina, but I notice tears in her eyes too. Nonna shakes her head and walks over to the office, returning with a big box of tissues. Joey comes in at one point and backs out, mumbling something about there being too much estrogen in the kitchen.

"Then he told me about himself." I refuse to repeat the story, telling Grace that she has to get it from Cooper or Sarah directly, which she says she will. Nonna rolls her eyes at this.

"So, how are you?" Fig asks.

I smile. "Okay," I say. And I am. Well, at least I'm better. A lot.

I take a deep breath and decide to remember this moment. This one is scented with cinnamon and filled with laughter and Fig's chatter.

"What now?" Fig asks. She looks down at her shoes. "Are you going back to Maine?"

"You can't get rid of me that easily," I say. It wasn't the easiest conversation to have with my father. My father was okay when I asked him if I could finish the summer. He was definitely disappointed, but he agreed that we should just take it slow. Let things grow *organically*. I smiled when he said that, making him laugh. He even called Nonna and spoke with her about it. Veronica was all for the idea, so much so that she started boxing up some of the books in my room so I can have more space.

Fig grins and twirls around the island toward the pot of strawberries she's supposed to be stirring.

"I can't wait until Saturday," Fig says, twirling back toward me. But then she gets all weird, like she just said something she shouldn't.

"What?" I ask, but Fig simply waves her fingers around as if batting away my question.

"I'm just excited," Fig says. I can tell something's up, but for once Fig manages to keep a secret. No amount of begging gets her to budge. She only hums and walks over to the stove to stir the big pot of jam again.

Nonna claps her hands. "Okay, break's over, everyone. Back to work!"

I start unwrapping the cream cheese for the Danish filling, and Nonna walks over beside me.

"I'm proud of you, Mia," she says. It's the kind of thing that sounds so lame coming from one of your parents, but coming from Nonna, it makes me feel all warm inside.

"Don't let it go to your head," Grace teases as she walks past. She gives me a smile before pushing through the door.

I turn on the mixer and watch the paddle smash the

cream cheese and sugar against the sides of the bowl. Fig starts singing off-key about moons and pie and amore. She twirls as she carries the pans of lasagna to the cooler. She then twirls over to me and pries me away from the mixer, taking my hands and twirling me around. Joey peeks back into the kitchen but immediately leaves again, telling us to call him when the lunacy is over. That makes Fig start laughing, and seeing her laugh makes me laugh too. Soon we're both laughing so hard we can't catch our breath.

I decide to get my camera to take a picture of me and Fig together, but then I remember I left it at Simon's place. But maybe some things can't be caught in a photograph. Things like the smell of fresh bread and the sound of laughter and that little glow inside your chest that suggests that maybe the heart that you thought was hard for good isn't.

"Where are we going?" I ask Cooper. I glance over at him, hardly believing he's with me. While I do prefer the jeans-and-T-shirt Cooper, he looks amazing in the tux he borrowed from one of Fig's cousins. Cooper told me he'd pick me up at Veronica's and we'd ride over to the MoMA together. We were going to ride the subway, but my dad said my dress was way too pretty to chance messing it up. *Take a cab,* he told me, pressing money into my hand.

"There's one there," I say, pointing to a taxi just letting a woman out a few cars away. Cooper shakes his head, and we keep walking. "Why do I get the feeling we're not going to the MoMA?" I ask.

Cooper only smiles at me and squeezes my arm.

"Not fair," I say.

"What's not fair?" he asks.

"You," I say. Cooper smirks.

"Did I already tell you how beautiful you look?" he asks. I blush like I did the first three times he said it.

"You did," I say. "Where are we going again?" I ask, trying for casual to see if I can trick him. Cooper only laughs.

The truth is, I don't really care where we're going, except that I should probably call my dad and Veronica if we aren't going to meet them on the steps in front of the museum like we'd planned. When I left, my dad was still trying to figure out how to knot his tie, refusing Veronica's help.

Cooper leads me down the street and over a block. "How're your feet doing?" he asks, nodding down at my new shoes.

"Good," I say. And it's only because Rina told Fig and me to wear our shoes around the house every day for half an hour at a time to break them in. Nonna yelled at us when we were wearing them in the kitchen, telling us they were unsafe.

We walk down one street and double back along the other side. "Do *you* know where we're going?" I ask.

"Trust me," Cooper says. We do the same thing on the next block. Finally, he turns toward the park.

"Wait," I say, realizing where we are going. "I thought

you said Simon wanted us to keep out because he had the floors done and no one could walk on them."

"He did," Cooper says. "But they're finished now."

We walk past the corner market, which has replaced its blueberries with a giant pyramid of canned peas. We draw even with Simon's, and I notice he's taken the paper off the windows—but it's dark inside, so you still can't see in.

"I told Simon we'd drop by to see the place," Cooper says. The sign on the door says *There* is closed for a private party. I start to tell Cooper that maybe we should come back, but he's already pulling the door open and nodding at me to go inside. It's really dark, even with some light coming in the windows.

"Don't be mad," Cooper says softly from behind me. Fig made me promise to wear my hair up, and Cooper's breath is warm on the side of my neck.

"Why would I be—"

The lights and the noise hit me at the same time. There are so many people yelling that I can't even hear what they're saying. Cooper takes my arm and draws me into the room. Everywhere I look, people are smiling at me. Fig is the first to rush toward me.

"Were you surprised?" she asks, taking my hands. I nod, suddenly unable to speak. "See?" she says to whoever can hear. "I kept the secret."

"Miracles will never cease," Grace says from off to one side, where she's standing with Gina and Nonna.

Sarah steps forward and hugs me. "Happy birthday," she says.

It's then that I see the banner stretched across the front of the room. *Happy 16th Birthday, Mia.* It's hard reading those words, realizing where I was a year ago. But then I remind myself of what Veronica said. Rachel would have wanted this for me.

Sebastian hugs me too. "I'm so glad you're finally here," he says. "I'm starving." I laugh.

My father waves at me from where he's standing with my grandmother, near the mural at the back. Cooper takes my hand and leads me through the crowded room. People I don't know keep stopping me and wishing me happy birthday. A few of them hug me.

"Who are all these people?" I ask Cooper.

He smiles. "Anyone you don't recognize is a Brunelli," he says. "Nonna insisted on inviting everyone. She said you deserved a real Brunelli birthday."

"Happy birthday, Mia-bird," my father says, putting his arm around me.

"How did you beat us over here?" I ask, but as soon as the question is out of my mouth, I know the answer. That was what all the walking was about. I narrow my eyes at Cooper, but he just grins at me.

"Happy birthday, Mia!" Simon calls from behind the counter. I wave as he hands another mug to someone I don't know and starts the next drink order. Sebastian, apparently too impatient to wait, has joined him. In between helping Simon make coffee, he's scavenging the trays of fruit sitting in front of him.

"This is really beautiful, Mia," my grandmother says, nodding toward the mural.

"Thank you," I say, putting my hand in hers. She gives me a triple squeeze and I feel my heart jump. When she nods and smiles at me, I blink away the tears that are threatening. "Cooper is the real artist," I say. "I pretty much just stood around in awe of his talent."

"We did it together," Cooper says, putting his hand on the center of my back. His hand is warm through the thin silk of my dress. "Look," Cooper says, pointing to the maple tree. He leads me toward the wall and touches one of the tiles that make up the leaves. There on a tile that might be *Sonora Sunset* or *August Flame* are three words: *Cooper and Mia.*

I lean against him. "You know those tiles are there forever," I say.

"I know," Cooper says. I feel my cheeks heating up.

"Attention!" Simon yells from where he's standing on a chair. "Mia! Please come here."

People step to one side to let me pass. When I reach Simon, he steps down from the chair, and then holds up a pie with candles sticking out of the top of it. Fig quickly lights each candle. I try to think of something to wish for, but looking around the room, I realize I have nearly everything I could hope for. Nearly.

"Get on with it!" Sebastian yells, making everyone laugh. "I'm hungry!" I take a deep breath and blow. No wish. Just air. Everyone claps as the last candle flutters out.

"Finally!" Sebastian yells, drawing more laughter. Simon, Nonna, and a few other Brunellis I still don't know start handing around pieces of pie.

I stand with Cooper, nibbling on my slice of lemon meringue. Sarah and Fig join us. Fig's is chocolate. Sarah's is apple. Sebastian walks up with a whole pie—blueberry—which he's eating right out of the pan with a fork.

"So," Fig asks. "Was this awesome?"

I nod. "What else is Simon going to serve here?" I ask.

Cooper shrugs. "Cake, cookies—dessert stuff. He said because Here serves breakfast, he wanted There to serve dessert."

"What about serving dessert for breakfast?" Sebastian asks. He takes another bite of his pie.

"There's one more surprise," Cooper says. He leads me over to a far wall, where something big hangs hidden under a cloth. Fig, Sarah, and Sebastian all stand nearby. "Close your eyes," Cooper says to me. I do. I feel air moving against my face as Cooper pulls the cloth free. Fig gasps from beside me. "Okay," he says. "Open them."

"Wow," Fig says.

"Amazing," Sarah says.

"This is good pie," Sebastian says. Fig laughs, but I barely notice.

Hanging in front of me is a collage of faces. All kinds of frames are tacked corner to corner: iron, silver, cherry, ceramic. Inside are Cooper looking out onto the water. Gina screaming after she was frightened by the magic wand.

Nonna sitting at her desk with her chin propped in her hand. Sarah with her eyes closed. Fig laughing. My dad smiling. My grandmother sitting in her chair, reading. And Rachel with her tongue stuck out. Then I see me. Cooper must have taken the photo when we were at Coney Island, because you can just see the edge of the Ferris wheel behind my shoulder. The wind is blowing my hair out of my face. My scar is clearly visible in the sunlight, but it's my eyes that keep me looking.

"I look happy," I say, softly. It's the first time I've really seen myself in a year. Cooper slides his hand into mine.

"Are you?" he asks.

"I am," I say, leaning into Cooper, so solid beside me.

"How did you get these from my camera?" I ask.

"You left it here, before—"

"The bridge and the rain and the *kissing*." I whisper this last word and I feel his laughter against my ear.

I turn to look at him and then at all the people crowded into the restaurant. My father is standing with Simon and laughing. My grandmother and Nonna are sitting together at a table and talking while they eat their pie. Sarah is being steered away from us by Grace and Gina, who are both fawning over her. Fig is laughing with Sebastian as he looks mournfully into his empty pie pan. Even Waffles is here, weaving in between legs and snatching up dropped crumbs.

"So, what did you wish when you blew out your candles?" Cooper asks.

"I can't tell you," I say. But it's not because I think that if I say it, it won't come true, but because it already has. I can feel my heart beating for the first time in a year. I know there will be places that will always hurt, but it's better to be hurt than to run from it like my mother did or to box it away like I tried to do.

Cooper puts his arms around me and pulls me toward him. I lean against his chest, feeling the starched fabric of his shirt on my cheek. "What now?" he asks.

"Everything," I say.

"Hmm," he says. "That's pretty wide open." I nod. I can feel the future opening up. Where there was just darkness, there are now points of light in front of me. "What do you want to do first?" he asks.

I glance around, noticing that everyone is talking and laughing together, and for the moment has forgotten about the two of us. "How about some of that *kissing*?" I ask, looking up at him.

"Yeah?" he asks.

"Yeah," I say.

He leans toward me. I close my eyes and feel his mouth on mine. There are people all around us, but for now all I can hear is the sound of my own heartbeat in my ears. Then I feel an insistent thumping on the backs of my legs. I pull back and look down at Waffles standing there. I smile at him and then up at Cooper, who is shaking his head.

"You're a mess," he says, reaching down and ruffling Waffles's ears.

I look down at Waffles's mournful eyes. "Don't worry," I say to him. "We're all a little messy." I think about all the people I know here. "I don't mind messy."

I peer up at Cooper again, and he's looking at me. And I feel it again: like he's really looking at me. Seeing me.

I hear my name and then Cooper's. Fig is near the mural, waving her hand at us. Simon has filled a table near the back with more pies. Sebastian and Joey and a couple of other guys—who, from the look of them, have to be Brunellis—are standing behind it.

"You want to watch?" Cooper asks, gesturing toward where Sebastian is standing with his hands clasped behind his back. I nod. Cooper takes my hand and pulls me forward. Waffles follows, his tail wagging the whole way as Cooper weaves past a sea of people I don't even know but who all know me. We stand off to the side, where we can see but won't get hit with flying pie.

"This is going to be messy," I say, looking at the rows of cream-covered pies on the table.

"I don't mind messy," Cooper says. He looks over at me and smiles.

"Get on with it!" someone yells from the other side of the room. I look over at Grace, who is standing on a chair so she can see over the crowd. Cooper steps behind me to let a stream of kids push past. He slides his arms around me and I lean back against him.

Simon is standing beside the table, looking at his watch, his hand raised. I think about my last birthday again and feel the ache in my heart. I know it will always be there. I touch my locket for a moment, thinking of the things inside: two grains of rice and a slip of paper. One grain is etched with Rachel's name. The other with Cooper's. They're like a bridge from one half of my life to the other. The other, a slip of paper—a predication of the future, or maybe just a pithy saying. *He who loves you will follow you.* I look over at my dad, standing with Veronica and laughing. I feel Cooper's arms around me. Then I feel a familiar weight on my foot and look down and see Waffles staring up at me.

"Ready?" Simon yells from where he's standing beside the table.

I smile. *As I'll ever be.*

The room gets quiet. The guys behind the table lean over their pies and I find myself holding my breath. The only noise is the rhythmic sound of Simon counting down from ten. When Simon yells *go,* the room fills with cheering; whipped cream goes flying; and I start breathing.

Acknowledgments

First, thank you to Erin Murphy of Erin Murphy Literary Agency, who always has a kind word when needed and a firm hand when called for. She navigates, leaving me free to enjoy the ride. I want to thank everyone at Blink for their kindness, support, and enthusiasm through many drafts, countless emails, and my move from Maine to Mexico to Texas. To Jillian Manning, who believed first. For Annette Bourland for championing this book. To Hannah VanVels for taking over the wheel. To Sara Bierling for helping me figure it all out. To Jacque Alberta for making sure I got it all right. (Any remaining mistakes are my own.) And to Sara Merritt and Jennifer Hoff for planning for tomorrow.

I must thank my amazing friends, Thomas and Alisa Simmons, for plying me with Albanese Sour Gummy Bears and always telling me I'm awesome (especially when I don't feel like it). And most of all thank you to my son, Harrison. You take my wild ideas, weird sense of humor, and impulsive road trips in stride. Thank you for making me want to be better than I am every day.

Teacher/Reading Group Discussion Questions

1. One of the most important relationships in *We Were Beautiful* is Mia's relationship with herself. What points in the narrative best illustrate her character growth and her ability to love and form friendships after her tragedy?

2. Mia has a very matter-of-fact, distinct voice. How are her emotions conveyed through her narrative voice?

3. What are a few ways the Brunellis impact Mia's idea of family and unconditional love? How are Nonna and Veronica foils to one another?

4. What are some key turning points in Mia's relationship with her grandmother? Can you identify places where Veronica starts to soften and warm to Mia?

5. One of the main romances in the story is between Mia and Cooper. How is it hinted that these two are kindred spirits right from their first meeting?

6. How does Cooper change after Mia comes into the story? Is there a turning point where closed-off Cooper becomes vulnerable Cooper?

7. In what ways is Mia's relationship different with each of her friends? In what unique ways do they each help Mia heal?

8. How does Mia come to terms with her sister's death, and why is this important to the story? How would you compare Mia at the beginning of the novel to Mia at the end of the novel?

9. What are the main takeaways from *We Were Beautiful*?

10. How can we as readers push back against the stigma surrounding ableism (discrimination against people with disabilities) and talk about it authentically?

Author Interview with Heather Hepler

What inspired you to write We Were Beautiful?

We Were Beautiful grew out of an idea that I had for a fairy tale—where a girl cursed from birth makes a decision that alters her appearance so drastically that her mother sends her away to live with her grandmother in another city. But after I started writing it, I realized that the story I really wanted to tell was about a girl in the real world who must deal with the same thing. In my fairy tale, there were all manner of possibilities—charms, witches, true love's kiss—but in the real world, magic isn't an option. Mia's story became the story I had to tell—a story of a girl who must learn to trust, to love, and to live again.

What do you hope readers take away from We Were Beautiful?

That forgiveness, love, and trust are all worth believing in and fighting for.

Tell us more about your main character, Mia.

Mia is my hero in so many ways. She has to walk through some very dark times, but she keeps going and hoping and believing. She finds a way to piece her life back together using art and her friends and her family. She also loves photography and kayaking and looking at the stars. And she has a special fondness for gingerbread-pumpkin whoopie pies.

Many of the characters in We Were Beautiful are aspiring artists. What draws each of them to their specific medium?

Fig is all about using art to draw people together. She believes that art should be interactive and social. She's fond of bright colors and large venues. She has thought about becoming an *extreme artist*, but when Sebastian presses her to explain what that is, she just says a lot of things about giant umbrellas and flash mobs and swimming pools full of lime Jell-O.

Sebastian sees himself as a performance artist. Competitive eating is really only a side hobby for him. He's currently designing plans for a life-size gingerbread house where he would actually live for a whole month. Fig already asked if she could play the part of the witch.

Sarah loves music. She can play the piano, the guitar, the sitar, a shofar, and the pan flute. The last three are thanks to the owner of Music World, who wants to bring new sounds to the NYC music scene. He also moonlights as a Foley artist, and believes that Sarah's ear for music is what gave her the idea for crushing up potato chips to make the sound of a crackling fire.

Cooper's biggest inspiration (aside from Mia) is nature, but to him even a small patch of grass between two trash cans can be beautiful. He also has a fondness for using unusual art materials. Lately he's been seen rummaging through the bins at Locks 'n' Clocks. He also has a large pile of PVC pipe stored in Simon's back room. When Mia asked him what he was working on, he just smiled.

Mia loves taking photographs. Her favorites are the close-ups of people's faces. She believes that everyone is beautiful; you just have to take the time to look.

Why do you think it's important for YA readers to meet characters like Mia, Cooper, Fig, Sebastian, and Sarah?

I think it's important to remember that everyone has a story. It's easy to just focus on the things we can see—beauty and wealth and status. But the important things are the things that you can't see, even the things we hide from each other. Mia and her friends have learned this. They support each other, love each other, and trust each other—even with the most painful parts of their stories.

What came first in this novel: characters or plot? Have you always known your main characters' story arcs or were there surprises along the way?

Mia was the first thing. I knew she was scarred, but I didn't know why. It wasn't until I began to write that I realized what had happened to her and her sister. I was surprised by Fig. Her personality just slammed into me and made me laugh. She's the kind of friend everyone should have, and everyone should be. The dogs that Cooper walks were another surprise. Now I can't imagine the story without them.

The friendship between Mia and Fig is a major theme in this story. What fictional or real-life friendships inspired your characters?

I tend to gravitate toward friendships with people who are my opposite. I'm quiet and shy. I prefer solitary hobbies like running and reading and baking bread. But my friends are all my opposites. They are all outgoing. They like to throw parties and join clubs and meet new people. I'm always drawn to friendships like Ron Weasley and Hermione Granger's, Frodo and Sam's, Meg Murray and Calvin O'Keefe's. You can't imagine one without the other.

Do you feel like your characters are your friends, or extensions of yourself? Which character do you feel resembles you the most? Which character do you wish you were more like?

Usually my characters are versions of myself or at least who I'd like to be. Mia is the most like me. She is reserved and quiet and likes pie. She also loves nature and likes to sit out in the cold and look at the stars. Fig is who I'd like to be. She is fearless and outgoing and always has a big plan. She also makes mistakes, says she's sorry, and moves on. Her confidence in herself and the love of those around her inspire me.

What is your favorite part of the writing process?

I love those moments where I go into what I call the *writing fog.* This is where the real world falls away and I'm in the story, watching it happening around me. In those moments, it feels less like creating a story and more like simply recording the story as it plays out.

How was the experience of writing We Were Beautiful different than writing your previous novels?

It was different mostly because I literally have eleven different drafts of it on my computer. The story morphs from a fairy tale story to what it is now in stages. It seems a lot like I took a recipe for angel food cake and made it eleven times, substituting one ingredient at a time until I ended up with chocolate chip cookies at the other end.

If you could tell your teen self anything, what would it be? What advice would you give a teenager today?

I would tell her to relax, enjoy life, and take chances. I'd also tell her that everything changes, but that's not a bad thing. I'd tell teenagers today the same thing. That and put down your phone—life isn't on that screen. (I have to tell myself that same thing sometimes.)

The setting of New York City is a rich part of Mia and her friends' story. What parts of the city inspired their stories?

When I'm in New York City, I walk everywhere. I'm afraid if I ride the subway, I'm going to miss something. Mornings always start with a trip to Zabar's for a bagel and fresh-squeezed orange juice. Then I go exploring. I love the tree-lined streets uptown and the funky shops in SoHo. And I love the bridges that tower over everything, inviting you to travel to new places. Museums are part of every trip. I love going to the Metropolitan Museum of Art with its Tiffany stained glass and huge marble sculptures. I also enjoy the MoMA and the American Museum of Natural History as well. And no trip would be complete without pizza and cupcakes, which are both featured in *We Were Beautiful*. I confess that I have yet to go to Coney Island, so the scene with Cooper and Mia was created with online research, but it's definitely on the list for my next trip.

Which part of We Were Beautiful *was the most challenging to write? What was your favorite scene to write?*

The most challenging scene for me to write was when Mia remembers everything from the night of the accident. I wanted to make sure it was clear that she was put in an impossible situation. I also wanted Mia to really experience it all over again. I think that moment is when she finally releases her pain and allows her heart to be open again. My favorite part was the scene at Coney Island. The beach, the Ferris wheel, the giant cotton candy, and of course Cooper. What could be better?

What does the title mean to you?

We Were Beautiful has a wistful quality to it. It's as if someone is remembering a time before an event when she was beautiful. But what I hope is that it will be clear by the end that they are all beautiful now and always will be.

How do you celebrate when you've finished writing a book?

It's always different, but when I finished *We Were Beautiful*, my son and I were living in a cabin on a lake in Maine (just like Mia and her family). We packed our dog into the car and drove into town. We bought pie (coconut cream) and then headed out to the beach to eat that pie, run around, and watch Daisy, our blue heeler, chase the waves.

Connect with Heather Hepler!

www.heatherhepler.com

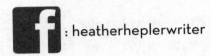 : heatherheplerwriter

 : @heatherheplerwriter

 : hlhepler

www.goodreads.com/author/show/121420.Heather_Hepler

Heather Hepler is the author of *Frosted Kisses* (Scholastic, 2015), *Love? Maybe* (Dial, 2012), *The Cupcake Queen* (Dutton, 2009), *Jars of Glass* (Dutton, 2008), *Dream Factory* (Dutton, 2007), and *Scrambled Eggs at Midnight* (Dutton, 2006). Heather has been making up stories in her head for as long as she can remember. It was an amazing day when she realized she could use her talent for good instead of evil. Now instead of making up outrageous stories to explain why her hands were dyed purple, what happened to the last cookie, or why she decided that spending twenty dollars on a talking fish was a good idea, she pours her creative energy into her novels, which she fills with whatever captures her attention: outer space, cupcakes, Renaissance Fairs, bacon truffles, Disney Princesses, sea glass, and love potions have all made the list. Currently she is fascinated with aliens and fruitcake. Her writing has received many awards and accolades, and she has been told more than once by her son that when she writes, she makes weird faces. You can contact Heather at cupcakequeen@heatherhepler.com.

BLINK